MW00386794

The Dead Squire

Prologue

The High Webinar led the little girl through the dank caverns beneath the castle keep. He held a torch in his left hand, and her small hand in his right. The wavering light glistened off of the damp walls of the tunnel, the torch popped and snapped like a flag on a windy day. Air moved through the caverns as if the castle were breathing. His heart beat so high in his throat that it threatened to choke him. He knew that this meant his certain death, just like he knew that the sun would rise tomorrow.

Shuffling through the gloom, he turned this way, then that, relying on his memory to get her to safety. He had fretted over the decision for as long as he dared, but in the end there was no one else to save her. It was him or no one. It was his life or hers. In the end the choice had been simple, much easier than the consequences, he feared. He was an old man, and not much longer for this earth. He would return to the World Wide Web, sooner rather than later, he knew. He could let the girl be murdered, and probably live a few more years, to die peacefully of old age, and go to Florida, or he could get her to safety and die now, painfully. The King's madness was surpassed only by his cruelty. The High Webinar had beared witness to this King's notion of justice, and the memory left him feeling ill.

"How much further," the little princess asked.

"We're almost there," he answered. "Just a little farther."

She was eleven, and the sweetest little girl he had ever met. She was also the true heir to the crown. As soon as she came of age, the King would have to step down. The High Webinar had learned that the King had no intention of doing that. The little princess would be killed, but it had to look like an accident. Poison wouldn't work, and this time being taken to work out the particulars gave him an opportunity to spirit her away.

At last he saw a dim light ahead. He picked up his pace as much as her little legs would allow. His spirits lifted as he began to make out the details of the figure ahead. She wore a dark cloak and carried a small lamp.

"Here we are," he said to the little girl.

The middle aged woman raised her lamp to get a better look at them. She had a kind face, he was relieved to see. Her brown eyes sparkled with intelligence in the lamplight.

"I'll…" she began.

"No," he cut her off. "Don't say anything. The less I know, the safer you two will be." It was true. He had no misconceptions about his own bravery and resolve. He would tell them everything he knew. The best he could hope for, is that they never even suspect him, but that was a slim arrow in the dark. He had a fly's chance of getting away with this. He let go of the girl's hand, and put his hand on her back, gently guiding her forward. The small boat rocked gently behind the cloaked savior.

"Come along now princess," she said, holding a hand out to the girl.

"Don't call her that anymore," the High Webinar said a little more forcefully than he had intended. "Give her a new name after I leave."

"Can I be Vantenia," the girl asked. That was the name of her favorite hero in the stories.

"No," he replied. "You must have a secret name that I don't know."

"Oh," she said, a little disappointed.

"Come along now," the lady said, holding out a hand toward the child.

The girl turned and looked up at the old man. "Do I have to go? I'm afraid," she said, young tears being birthed in her eyes.

"Yes, I'm afraid so," he said, squatting down and cupping her cheek in a wrinkled hand. "You must be brave, just like Vantenia. This is your story, and you must make it a good one."

He felt tears burning his own eyes as she unexpectedly wrapped her little arms around his neck and squeezed.

"They're going to hurt you," she said. It was a statement of fact.

"I'll be careful," the old man said, trying to ease her mind.

"It won't matter," said the princess.

The little girl let go and ran to the boat, as if afraid she might change her mind if she took the time to walk. He watched the cloaked woman help the little girl into the boat. She untied it, and hopped in, then pushed away from the stone dock without a word. He stood there as they disappeared into the darkness, tears running freely down his bony wrinkled cheeks. He didn't know if he was crying for the girl or for himself, maybe a little of both.

The girl's words worried him. He knew that he had to do this, that he didn't really have a choice, and he was willing to pay the consequences for his actions, but he held onto a small glimmer of hope, that he would get away with it. The princess had just dimmed that little light. He shook his head, trying to clear away the unwanted thoughts. The Weaver weaved the web, what was done was done, and what would be done, would be done.

At last he turned, heading back the way they had come. He took his time. He was in no hurry to meet his fate.

Chapter One

Alek was a young man who lived with his mother, his Uncle Remi, and his Aunt Tilda in the small village of Brookville. Just now, he was sitting at his uncle's table listening to his mother fret.

"I can't believe you Alek," she said. "That was the third job this month. Your uncle Remi is going to be so upset." She stood in the kitchen, arms crossed under her breasts, the light from the window behind her, reduced his mother to a dark silhouette. He looked down at the table that his uncle had built, pretending to be interested in the wood grain. A woodpecker was tapping on a tree outside, and he could hear Strand the sheep bleating in the backyard.

"I did everything he told me to do. I don't know what else he expected from me," Alek said. This was more or less true. He had done what the smith had told him to do, but no more. Smithing was hot, boring work, and Alek couldn't force himself to enjoy it, or show interest.

"There is more to it than that. Old Pate wouldn't dismiss you for no reason. You pulled some stunt, or smarted off, I'd just *bet*! And you are going to be in deep trouble when your uncle gets back. He is going to be spun!"

Alek slapped the table with both hands, and stood so fast that the chair fell over behind him. "You and uncle Remi can *both* get tangled!" he yelled. The look of surprised pain on his mother's face sucked the anger right out of him. He looked back down at the table, wishing that he could have the words back. His hands stung from the slap he had given it, and the door opened with a bang. Both of their heads jerked toward it in surprise. Instead of the angry uncle he had expected, Alek saw two large men in scale armor standing in the doorway.

The one on the left pointed at him and said, "You, come with us." The other one walked toward him, and began to motion him to the doorway. His mother began to wail.

At first he just looked at them, not understanding. *Are you talking to me,* he thought. When the man reached him, he found his voice, "What is this about?"

"You've been drafted into Lord Bracken's militia," the man said.

"Come along now lad," the other one said, still standing in the doorway.

His mother continued to cry as he walked toward the door. He didn't know what else to do. There was only one egress in the house, he couldn't run, and they both had swords, so fighting was out of the question. Plus, he had known this could happen. It was not unheard of, uncommon maybe, but not unheard of.

His mother finally began to speak. "Not again," she screamed, "Please don't take my boy! The Mother curse you bastards, don't take my booooooooy," she wailed as she followed them out the door.

Once outside Alek saw a small gathering in the street. Two more young men about his age, Mar the Liar and Tesson, were standing in the middle of the hard dirt street, surrounded by a dozen armed men. Mar was called "The Liar" to differentiate him from the other Mar who lived on a farm outside the village. He had earned that specific tag by never being outdone. If you caught a six inch trout from Lady Creek, Mar would tell you of the seven inch trout he caught last month. If you jumped from a rock into the water, he would tell you about the time he had jumped from a higher rock. Their mothers were also crying and pleading. Having some company made Alek feel a little better. Though, he had no idea why having more people share his fate would do that. By all rights, he should feel worse.

One of the soldiers was on horseback, and he said "Is that it?"

A chorus of yes's and yeah's answered him.

"Well, let's move out," he said.

As his little group neared the bigger one, it occurred to Alek to say goodbye to his mother. He turned around and looked over his captor's shoulder, and saw her sitting near uncle Remi's front porch, with her head in her hands, sobbing. Even if he had yelled, she wouldn't be able to hear him over the other mothers wailing and soldiers talking. He turned back around at the urging of the man trailing him. Tesson's mother was physically being held back by a couple of the soldiers, while she struggled to reach her son. As he joined the other two boys, the entire group started to move down the street.

"What's going on," Mar asked.

"We've been drafted," Tesson answered.

Both of them looked frightened. Tesson looked around as if caught in a trap, and Brista looked wide eyed at Alek.

"I reckon some lord or other needs us to fight in his spinning war," Alek said.

One of the soldiers who was close enough to overhear, turned to him and said, "It's Lord Bracken, and I'd keep a civil tongue in my head, if I were you." It wasn't said roughly or unkindly, just friendly advice. Still, Alek heard the steel under the velvet veneer.

They walked along in silence for a time. All lost in thought. Then Mar spoke up, "When do you think we'll be able to go home?" They all just looked at each other. No one had any idea what the answer may be, next week, next month... never?

The thought of running occurred to Alek. He looked at the men around him. About half of them had crossbows and one of them was mounted on a swift looking horse. Alek wasn't an expert on horse flesh, but he could see the muscles in the animal's legs as it walked. He knew that he had a fly's chance of outrunning the beast. That plus the thought of a crossbow bolt in his back, kept his feet from itching too much. He kept walking, and thinking.

It occurred to him that the last words he had spoken to his mother had been curses, not I love you, I will miss you, or even goodbye. He had cursed her and his uncle. *Why stop there? Why didn't you curse your aunt Tilda too? If you're going to be a fool, you might as well be a full fool.* He felt shame and regret gnawing in his belly. His last action at home had been to curse those that loved him the most. Something else was bothering him though. Something was buzzing in the back of his mind, like an insect in a web, but just out of reach.

"I miss my ma," Tesson said.

"Yeah, I miss *your* ma too," Mar answered with a forced grin.

No one laughed at the dusty attempt at humor. Tesson just looked down at his feet, and kept walking.

"I'm sorry," Mar said. "I miss my ma too. I wonder if she'll be ok. I really hope that we get to go back pretty soon. Hey, maybe they just need our help for one fight or something. That would be great. What do you guys think?"

Neither of them answered, both lost in thought. *That was it*, Alek thought. His mom had said, "Not again!" At the time, he was too preoccupied to pay attention, but it came back to him now. What had she meant by that? She couldn't have had another son, could she? She must have been talking about his father. She had never been forthcoming when he asked her about his father. Alek knew that his father had died when he was a baby, but not much more. He hadn't fared much better when he had asked his uncle Remi. Remi said that his mother would tell him in her own time, and it wasn't his place to interfere. There were a lot of unanswered questions when it came to Alek's father, he didn't even know his father's name. That had to be it though, right? What else could she have meant?

They walked for many hours, past fields, meadows, and forests. They stopped once, to rest, by a stream with clear cool water. Alek had never tasted anything so good. He was thirsty, and his legs were numb from walking. The cold water splashing across his tongue and down his throat felt grand. He sat down at the edge of the road and massaged the big muscles in his thighs. His feet ached, but there wasn't much he could do about that. No one talked, the only sounds were splashes, grunts, and sighs of relief.

After about 20 minutes, the leader, Alek supposed, since he rode the horse, called for them to get moving. It was late in the afternoon by the time they finally reached the camp, weary and hungry. The campsite sprawled on either side of the road, and held several hundred men. At the far side was a wagon and a large canvas tent. Several dozen fires burned. The leader dismounted and handed the reins to another man, then motioned for the boys to follow him.

"You three, come with me."

He led them to an old man who was bellowing at a line of young men that were holding shields and spears.

"I got three more for ya Cal," the leader said.

The old man eyed the newcomers and said, "You bring me turds and expect me to cook award winning chili." His voice was wet gravel. "It ain't gonna happen. I'll do what I can with this lot, but don't expect them to do anything right, except piss themselves." He looked back at the three boys. "Well," he said pointing to a pile of shields and spears off to his left, "grab a shield and a poker, and get in line."

They did as commanded, too tired and scared to argue, and on some level they knew that they needed this training, if they were going to have a chance to stay alive.

"Alright, I'll start from the beginning, seeing as how we only been going for a few minutes anyway, and we got three new turds," the old man said. "I'm Sir Calder Spearman. You will call me Sir Calder. You will keep your ears open and your mouths shut."

After drilling with spear and shield for several hours, the boys were finally fed and allowed to pick out a soft patch of ground and go to sleep. They were too exhausted to start a fire. Even after so much had happened, sleep found them quickly.

Chapter Two

Alek woke the next morning with a boot in his ribs. "Get up," said a faceless voice in the dark. Alek opened his bleary eyes and sat up. His back, legs, feet, and arms rose up in a chorus of paint and protest. He had never been so sore in all his life. Satisfied that Alek was awake, the man moved on to the next. "Get up," Alek heard him say.

Once the waker had all three boys standing around him, he introduced himself. "I am Sir Calemy Stronghand," he said. "I am your new rank leader. There are five ranks under Lord Bracken's command, and we are rank three. Your sole purpose in life is to do what I tell you to do," he said. "Follow me."

With that, Sir Calemy turned on his heel, and strode off through the gloom. It wasn't easy to keep up. As they walked through the camp, Alek saw men in different stages of waking and preparing for the day. He noticed that no one had lit a fire. Sir Calemy finally stopped at a group of about a dozen men, and turned to face the boys.

"This is third rank," he said, gesturing to the men standing behind him. "You will eat with them, march with them, sleep with them, and fight with them. And if you are smart, you will learn from them," he said, and strode off, leaving them standing there facing 12 grizzled strangers, in the dark.

"Well, what do we have here," said one man, in a mocking voice, as he took a step toward the boys.

"Shut up Cholt," another said. "We don't have time for screwin' around this mornin' and I don't want to hear it. We've got to get to the chuck wagon before it leaves, if we're gonna to get anythin' to eat." He started waving his hands at the whole group, as if herding chickens. The other men began picking up packs of belongings from the ground and moving in the direction he was waving, Cholt muttering under his breath, but did as he was commanded.

They all moved off in single file. The three boys were last, and the one in charge fell in behind them. Their small line met a bigger one at the chuck wagon, and the walking stopped. While they waited, the man behind them said, "I'm Fenner. I'm in charge of third rank when Sir Calemy is not around. If you need to talk to Sir Calemy, you come to me first. I'm your mother, your father, and your uncle, but I'm not your friend. Remember that."

"Where are we going," Tesson asked.

"We're goin' where Lord Bracken says go," Fenner replied. "That's all you need to know."

Before long, they were at the chuck wagon, accepting their portions of bread and cheese. They ate on the move, following the men in front of them. The sun was beginning to rise, and Alek could see the column of men stretching off into the distance ahead. It struck him how naive he had been. When he had thought of knights and soldiers, he thought of honor, glory, and gold. Living the truth was a boring, and sobering ordeal.

As he walked and ate, his mind went again to his mother. That thing she had said, "Not again," it haunted him. He had always been curious about his father. The thing was, he really believed his mother. She had loved his father, and it hurt her to talk about him. She would have told Alek eventually, he was sure. Still, her having a good reason for not telling him never filled the hole in his heart. If his father had been drafted into Lord Bracken's service, maybe Alek could find out about him from the soldiers here. He made up his mind to ask some questions the next time they make camp.

And they walked. And walked. And walked.

The dreary, painful, boredom of a long march is unmatched in the realms of men. It was like volunteering to be tortured. Alek's feet were blistered and they screamed at him with every step. His legs had stopped being sore, they were oddly numb. His own head had become heavy. It was difficult to keep it up. He kept finding himself staring straight down at his feet. They stopped to rest at mid morning, and again at lunch. After the lunch break they filed past the wagon, got their ration of salt pork and bread, and again ate on the move.

At midafternoon, Alek was plodding along, putting one foot in front of the other, when he saw a man from in front of the line, falling back, limping. The man was a veteran. Until then, it never occured to Alek that he could stop. He could fall back, just sit down in the road. What was stopping him? The unknown stopped him. He had no idea what they did with men who couldn't make the march. The punishment for not marching could be a lot worse than marching. Another reason was Mar and Tesson. He couldn't fall out before them. If they could march, so would he.

After what seemed an eternity, they arrived at camp. The head of the column had already been there awhile. Alek noticed campfires already burning. Their small group peeled off the main force, and made its way to Sir Calemy.

"This is our area," he said, pointing at the ground. "New guys, meet Sir Calder over there in one hour," he said, raising his pointed finger to a small clearing on the other side of the dirt road. He looked at Fenner and said, "I'll be at the pavilion if I'm needed," and strode away.

Fenner ordered the three boys to go to the wagon and see if they had any bedrolls for them. By the time they had received their bed rolls and laid them out in the third rank area, it was time to meet Sir Calder. As they walked, they saw new recruits from all over camp, heading that way. When they got there, and Sir Calder was sure that everyone was present, he had them all sit down. Alek grunted with relief when he sat down, and it was echoed by almost everyone else. They were all glad to be off their feet.

Sir Calder remained standing, and began to pace back and forth in front of them.

"There's three kinds of fighting," he began. "The first is rodeo fighting. You can fight another man, or a bull, or a horse, but it's all the same. Does anyone know the most important thing about rodeo fighting?"

One young man raised his hand, and Sir Calder nodded to him. "Winning," he said.

"Good try, but no," the old man said. "Honor is the most important thing when fighting like that. Many's the time I saw a man turn down the champion's purse because of honor. The second kind of fighting is gutter fighting. It's dirty and savage, whether against a bear in the woods or another man in a tavern. There's no crowd to impress and no honor to lose. What is the most important thing about this kind of fighting," The old man asked again.

The same young man raised his hand, and again Sir Calder nodded to him. "Killing your foe."

"Again, good try, but no," Sir Calder replied. "In gutter fights, you just have to survive. Would you really care if the bear ran away? The same goes for the man in the tavern. What if he just stopped fighting and ran away? It doesn't matter how you do it, but staying alive is the only reason you are fighting. What both of these two types of fighting have in common, is that they are usually against one foeman. You are focused on one enemy, and whatever he is trying to do," he said. "The last type of fighting is the kind that we do. We do battle with armies. Can any of you tell me what the most important thing is about this kind of fight?"

No one offered a suggestion.

"Killing," Sir Calder said. "Your job is to kill them. If we put more of them in the ground, than they do us, we win. I have seen lots of gutter fights and rodeos where no one died, but I haven't seen one single battle like that.

Some of us are going to die, but live or die, if we kill enough of them, we win. We protect our families and small folk by killing. Make no mistake," he wagged a bony finger at them. "There's some gold and glory to be had on a battlefield, but naught of honor. Where's the honor in laying in the mud, and shoving your blade between a man's ribs, as you watch the life drain from his face? Where's the honor in that? He's got a family too, and he believes that he is fighting for the right, just like you. Do you know who's right, boys? Do ya? It's very simple. No matter what cause they defend, or who they are protecting, or what gods they honor, the better killers are always right on the battlefield. The Web and the gods always, *always* side with the best killers."

"Also," he went on, "when fighting in a battle, your attention can't be focused on a single enemy. You must be aware of everything that is going on around you at all times. It's what you don't see that will kill you. Remember that. A mace to the back of the head will kill you just as quick, if it's swung by one of your allies." "Be prepared to be hated. It will flat rattle some folks to see pure hatred for them in the enemies eyes. They've got to hate you enough to feel ok about cutting your heart out, and you have to feel the same about them. Hatred is the fuel of battle, like wood for a fire. Find a reason to hate your enemy. Them trying to kill you is enough reason for most."

With that, he walked them over to the supply wagon, to get them outfitted with proper spears and shields. Alek's spear was in good shape. It had a long maple shaft and the blade wasn't rusted too badly. His shield was heavy, but strong, made of oak and iron. He hefted them both to get the feel. Afterward, they returned to their area, ate, and slept. The bed rolls were more comfortable than the cold ground, and they were completely exhausted. Just before he fell asleep, Alek remembered that he had planned to ask questions about his father. He would have to do that tomorrow, he needed sleep.

Alek dreamed of his mother. She cried as he cursed her. Tears ran down her face as she begged him not to go. His uncle was there, yelling at him for losing another job. He ran for the door, then stopped and turned around. They were both dead, lying in pools of blood. Now Sir Calder was standing in the corner, his wrinkled face stretched around a large smile. "Your job is to kill them," he whispered. "You are a killer."

A different boot, a different morning, but the aches and pains were the same. Alek sat up as Fenner finished waking up the rest of the rank. Once everyone was up, and he had their attention, Fenner said, "There was a rider in the night. The enemy is close, we go to battle this morning. Leave everything here, except spear and shield."

Alek's heart began to hammer in his chest. Battle? It's really going to happen? What if he died without getting to apologize to his mother? Was it going to hurt? He didn't really fear death, he knew that he was safe in the Web, but he dreaded the thought of his body being punctured or mangled. If he had to die, he hoped that it would be quick and painless.

As he stood from retrieving his spear from the ground, someone bumped into him, hard. He nearly fell. Chote? Was that his name? The same guy who started to harass them the other day, and was silenced by Fenner. He had made a few more remarks since then, but Alek had been too tired to pay any attention. What was his problem? Whatever it was, now was not the time to find out. Alek swallowed his angry words and continued to prepare.

The entire camp moved in silence. Almost no one spoke above a whisper, as they began to march out in single file. They marched for several hours, and dawn was just breaking when they came upon a bethel of the Web. The religious building looked a lot like the Blue Bethel back home. Alek had never known why it was called "Blue Bethel," it wasn't blue. He could see who he assumed to be Lord Bracken, on horseback, forming up the ranks in front of the building. He was pointing and giving directions. Sir Calemy came walking up from the Lord's direction.

"Fenner," Alek heard him say.

"Here," Fenner said.

"We have the right side. Form them up on that end. Do it quickly."

"Aye Sir," Fenner responded, and turned around to give orders. They moved quickly across the field and lined up on the far side. They stood there for a while, just waiting. The rustling of garments and the clank of gear were the loudest sounds. At one point someone came out of the bethel and spoke to Lord Bracken, then scurried back inside.

The enemy did arrive though. They came straight down the road that was blocked by Lord Bracken's troops. They stopped about 100 yards away and formed up. The enemy was outnumbered, but not by much. The enemy leader rode out to meet Lord Bracken between the two armies. They spoke for several minutes, Lord Bracken shaking his head, while the other man gestured and gesticulated wildly. Finally the both rode back to stand beside their bannermen behind the infantry line.

Alek heard Lord Bracken yell, "Forward!" The order was echoed by the five knights who led each rank. The whole army began to move forward as one. Everything that he had been taught by Sir Calder was flying through Alek's mind. His hands were slick and sweaty as he moved them to improve the grip on his spear and shield. He watched as the enemy line advanced toward him. Their banner was close enough to see now, and he saw that it was the royal sigil of house Waters. Probably the only banner with which he was familiar. It was *the* spinning *King's* banner! His mouth went dry and he suddenly needed to shit, badly.

When they were about 10 feet from the enemy, the kingsmen charged. Alek raised his shield and braced for the impact. The man directly in front of him swung a mace in a swift arc. Alek felt it beat against his shield, but he remembered Sir Calder's advice, and looked to his right. The kingsman there was focused on the ally to Alek's right. While keeping half of his attention on the man swinging the mace at him, he thrust his spear at the exposed neck of the man on the right. It wasn't a direct hit, but his spear cut a deep furrow in the back of the kingsman's neck. The foe to his front suddenly went down and it allowed him a brief second for another thrust. This one was true. He felt his spear stop, when it met the man's spine. The kingsman dropped as if his legs had been removed. The gap was still empty in front of him, so Alek moved his attention to the enemy at his left. Alek was on the defended side of this foe, a shield was in his left hand, but he could help keep him occupied while someone else dealt the killing blow. And so it went. The man turned toward Alek, raising his halberd, and took a foot of steel in the armpit for his trouble. With no one left to fight, Alek stepped out to have a look, and saw that the enemy down the line, were busy running or dying.

He looked down at the man he had killed, and noticed his shield. It looked strange. He picked it up and noticed right away that it was much lighter than his own. His companions were walking away, uninterested, so he picked up the halberd dropped by the other man, as well. It had a 6 foot hickory shaft, with a small ax head on top. Sprouting from the top of the ax was 18 inches of steel spear head. His first spoils of battle. He felt good, alive for maybe the first time in his life. He had just killed a man, and wasn't going to be punished for it. He liked the *feeling* of battle. Life and death balanced on a knife's edge. No amount of boot licking or ass kissing could aid a man in a shield wall. You had your wits and your strength, and at the end you were alive, or not. It was true, clean, and powerful. At this moment, he could not imagine living any other way. How could a man go from this to being a cobbler or farmer?

As he stood there admiring his halberd, Lord Bracken rode up, surveying the line corpses. He reined in, dismounted, and held the reins out toward Alek.

"Hold my horse," he said.

Alek reached out and took the reins. Lord Bracken ducked under his horse's neck and went to one of the fallen men. He knelt beside him, then reached out and closed the man's eyes in a way that was both affectionate and kind. He placed his open hand over his heart in the sign of the Web, and began to recite the prayer. Alek couldn't hear the words, but he didn't have to. He knew it.

"May you be untangled, and the Weaver spin you anew.

May you know the Mother's love and live again.

The Father guide you to your next home in the Web.

You will be missed in this one."

He stood slowly, turned, and looked at Alek. "My squire is dead. Follow me," he said in a flat hollow voice, and strode off, not bothering to check to make sure that his order was being followed.

Chapter Three

Alek followed, leading the horse past the line of dead men. He had imagined that the sight of the dead would bother him more than it did. Several of the living soldiers were claiming their winnings from the dead, as he had done a few moments ago. Most of them were in a group surrounding the prisoners, and that is where Lord Bracken was headed now. Alek led the horse close enough to overhear the conversation.

"Balto," Lord Bracken said, he seldom gave his knights the honorific "Sir" while out in the field, "you and the first rank, take the prisoners to the keep, and return as fast as you can. They will be treated with decency, but they will not escape." Lord Bracken never told anyone what he wanted to be done, or what he expected, he simply explained what *would* happen.

"Yes, my lord," Balto replied. He spun and yelled, "First rank, to me!" Men looked up from their looting and came running over.

Lord Bracken left them to it, and began walking toward the bethel, Alek followed. A man in white robes stood by the door. When he saw Lord Bracken coming toward him, he left the doorway to meet him. The holy man was average size, but he looked small next to Lord Bracken, who took up a lot of space. The nobleman was almost a foot taller than the webinar and 40 or 50 pounds heavier. He didn't wear the usual paunch that most men his age seemed to favor. The black scale mail that he wore was of the highest quality, and expensive, but worn from use. The dark mail made the webinar's robes seem even brighter by contrast.

"My lord," he said. "You have saved us from certain death, the Weaver love you."

"Do you know why they came here," the lord asked.

"No milord," the webinar replied, shaking his head vehemently. "We had heard that the King's men were burning places of worship and slaying the faithful within, but we have no idea why, none at all milord."

Lord Bracken only grunted at this and looked over the webinar's shoulder at the bethel. "Do you mind if I have a look inside?" The question was a courtesy, and a formality. The man could not very well deny him access while he had an army at his back, an army that had just saved them.

"Of course milord," the webinar said, bowing slightly and extending an arm toward the bethel.

Lord Bracken walked past him, giving Alek the briefest of glances and motioning for him to stay. Alek watched them go and began to talk to the horse softly. He had always talked to animals as if they were people, he got that from his mom, he supposed.

"Me and you are going to be buddies, aren't we," he said while scratching the animal's neck. "I'll find you something good to eat as soon as we're done here."

Alek surveyed the battlefield while he talked to the horse. He saw some members of third rank among the milling men, including Tesson, but he could not locate Mar. It struck him that Mar could have been killed. There were a few casualties on their side, including the squire, it seemed. He and Mar had never been close, he wouldn't consider Mar a friend, but he felt a small bolt of fear blow through him at the thought of the other man's death. Maybe it shined a light on his own mortality, or maybe he felt closer to the guy than he cared to admit. Did Lord Bracken mean to make him a squire? He had always thought that squires were highborn. No, the Lord just needed someone to hold his horse. He was letting his imagination run away with him. Squires and knights didn't rise from lowborn soldiers like him.

That's when he noticed one of the figures was standing still, staring at him. It was Chote. He stood still, the butt of his spear on the ground, his shield dangling from his left hand, looking directly at Alek. What was his problem? Alek hadn't done anything to the man that he could remember. Alek hadn't had time to offend anyone. He'd probably spoken five words since he had arrived that first evening. He looked back at the man for several seconds, not wanting to be the first to look away, in the way that men had of being afraid to look afraid.

"Let's go," Lord Bracken's voice startled him.

The lord walked past him, and he followed, leading the buckskin gelding behind him.

"Calemy," Lord Bracken yelled. Sir Calemy turned and jogged toward them, his chain armor clinking with each step.

"Yes my lord."

"Get the spoiling done and get everyone back to camp. The diggers are on their way," the lord ordered. A good thing too, Alek thought, he could see buzzards starting to wheel overhead. The diggers would bury the dead after cleaning them of anything valuable.

The moment he was sure that his order was understood and would be obeyed, Lord Bracken turned to Alek and took the reins from his hand. He mounted and looked down at the young man. "You will meet me at my pavilion as soon as you return." With that, he rode off the way they had come earlier that morning.

Alek was unsure whether he should follow, or find Fenner, and ask him. That thought reminded him of Mar, and made his decision for him. He began to look for either Mar or Tesson. It didn't take him long to locate Tesson. He was milling around with a dazed look on his face.

"Tesson," Alek said. The young man looked up at the sound of his name and Alek saw a gash across his left cheek, just under the eye. Tesson's eyes lit up a little at the sight of a familiar face, and he raised his chin in acknowledgement. "Where's Mar?"

Tesson pointed with his spear at a pile of corpses. "I think he's there now. After spoiling them for loot, they just piled them there."

Alek felt a tinge of guilt at his own spoiling. He was happy to have his shield and halberd though, and he was a realist. This was war, and he would do what he had to to survive. The Web and the Weaver took care of the dead, the dead had no use for mortal tools. The living however...

Should he pray for Mar, as Lord Bracken had done for his squire? He didn't relish the thought of digging through that pile of corpses for his acquaintance, the webinars would probably pray for the dead anyway. They were right outside a bethel. He took some comfort in that thought. Mar had died defending a bethel. The gods and the Web could not ask for a better death. Mar would definitely be spun out again, as a highborn noble, feasting and fighting in glory and honor.

"Form up," the sharp command took the decision away from him. Alek got into formation with the rest of the men. Tesson was directly in front of him on the march back to camp. The young man walked using his spear as a cane and with his shield hanging limply at his side.

"You ok," Alek asked him.

"Yeah, I'm just tired," Tesson replied, but Alek could tell it was more than that. Tesson had always been a cheerful fellow, the joy of life that was the mark of his personality, seemed to have been leached out of him. What really nagged at Alek though, was his own reaction to the situation. He knew that Tesson was probably behaving normally under the circumstances. He had just killed a man, after all, and lost a comrade. It occurred to him to ask Tesson if he had been bloodied, but the question was probably in bad taste, considering the other man's dark mood. They walked in silence for a bit, listening to the snatches of conversation from the other soldiers.

"The King has lost his rocks," one man swore. "He's burning bethels all over the realm. Thinks he's the spinning Weaver!"

"Yeah," said another, in a conspiratorial tone. "Lords Holt and Bracken will set things a'right though."

"Well," said a third, "if the King wants to keep sending us these poachers and debtors, I'll keep killing them." A chorus of laughter and agreement followed.

Poachers and debtors? What in the web did that mean? They looked like soldiers to Alek. He supposed that he could not tell the difference between a soldier and a thief though, and it didn't take hardened veterans to burn a bethel full of unarmed webinars. This morning, the march to the bethel seemed to take forever, but the march back was done almost as soon as it began.

Alek stepped out of line and started toward the pavilion, but he was stopped by a knight whose name was unknown to him.

"Where are you going," the knight asked.

"Lord Bracken told me to report to his pavilion when I got back," Alek said.

The knight looked him up and down. "You're Eleven huh? Alright, you'd better get along then." The night ignored Alek's look of confusion, turned to the line of soldiers, and started barking orders.

Alek made his way to the pavilion, wondering what the knight had been talking about. The buckskin gelding was tied to a hitching post still wearing his gear. Alek gave him a pat as he walked by. Alek didn't consider himself a horseman, but he knew enough to make his presence known before walking behind the animal. A startled horse could lash out with his hind legs, and kill a person without thinking.

Lord Bracken was standing just inside the pavilion talking to Sir Calemy. Alek stopped a polite distance away and waited. The lord noticed him and said, "Untack Wog and hobble him around back. Get some hay from the chuckwagon and feed him. Master Wayne knows how much to give him."

Alek turned without a word and did as instructed. Wog? A wog was a vicious wild animal that was supposed to be related to the domestic dog, or so Alek had learned. The name didn't fit this mild mannered beast. The gelding was friendly and affectionate, though most likely trained for war. He could be vicious on the battlefield, Alek supposed. He had been too involved in his own fight to see the gelding in action.

He got the tack removed and led the horse around back. There he found the hobbles and some hay left over from the last time Wog was fed. The animal began to eat, but otherwise stood still while he was hobbled. As he was walking back to the front of the pavilion he heard Lord Bracken calling, "Eleven, Eleven!"

Confused, Alek looked through the opening. Lord Bracken noticed him and said, "There you are." He came out, and pointed to some bedding on the ground next to the large tent. "You sleep here, unless it's raining," and it dawned on Alek that he was looking at the bedding of the dead squire, "then you sleep inside. Are you finished with Wog?"

"No milord, I still have to get the hay. Do we have a brush?"

"Get one from Wayne, and let me know when you're done."

"Yes milord." Alek moved off toward the wagon. Eleven? That's the second time he had been called Eleven. What did that mean? He found master Wayne at the wagons, eating a pickled egg.

"Lord Bracken sent me for hay and a brush," he said to the small man.

"So, you're Eleven huh," the man said.

"What does that mean," Alek asked. "You're the third person to call me that."

"Lord Bracken doesn't have much luck with squires," Wayne replied with a humorless chuckle. "The first ten are all dead. You are number eleven."

Chapter Four

Alek was almost in a trance as he brushed Wog. The big gelding chewed his hay placidly and paid him no mind. Squire? Squire! A squire was nobly born. Squires became knights. Everything had happened so fast. It seemed like yesterday that he had been sitting at his uncle's table, listening to his mother. It hadn't been yesterday, had it? It also felt like forever. His mother was a distant memory from another life. Would she be proud of him if she knew? Probably, but mothers were proud of everything. He hadn't done anything to earn her pride, had he? He *had* killed a man, but would she be proud of that? He knew that she would be proud of him for becoming a squire, but he knew that it was luck more than anything that had earned him the honor. He had been in the right place at the right time. He certainly didn't feel pride for killing that man, did he? He didn't feel shame though. He thought that he should feel some negative emotion after killing another human being, but he didn't. This worried him. Alek had actually *enjoyed* the fight. Tesson seemed to be shaken up by the experience, and Mar didn't survive it. Thinking about Mar's death, he thought that he should feel... *more*. More something, but it wasn't there.

There was also the fact that they had fought against the King's men. That worried and upset him. He had always thought that soldiers fought bandits, canables up north, and occasionally cowfolk. He thought that soldiers fought *for* the King, not against him. Why were kingsmen attacking the bethel? It was right to protect the bethel, Alek knew that for sure. It might be the only thing he was sure of.

"Levin," a voice said from behind him, apparently "Eleven" was too much to say. He had been too lost in thought to notice the approach amid the other camp sounds.

Alek turned toward the voice, but kept brushing. "Yes, Sir..." he trailed off.

"Sir Varn, if you please." The knight was tall and slim, and moved with a cat's grace. He wore a friendly smile, and pointed to Alek's new shield that he had leaned against the pavilion. "Would you like to sell that," he asked.

The question took Alek by surprise. "Sell it," he repeated stupidly.

"Yes," the knight said, and motioned to the shield. "Do you mind?"

"No, go right ahead."

Sir Varn picked up the shield and admired it. "Cowfolk shields are hard to come by. This isn't the best one I've seen, but it's the real thing. How much do you want for it?"

Alek noticed Cholt stop in the distance to stare at him. Anger and fear flared up inside him in equal portions. What in the Web was this guy's problem?

"Well," the knight interrupted his thoughts.

"No," Alek said, shaking his head. "I don't think I want to sell it, just yet." He had more sense than to sell something when he had no idea of its value. The knight's interest alone, spoke volumes about the shield.

"Ok. If you change your mind, come find me ok? Sir Varn," the knight reminded him.

"Sure thing," Alek said as the knight sat the shield back.

Alek looked up again, but Cholt was gone. He watched Sir Varn walk away and something tickled at the back of his mind. The man had shown him an awful lot of courtesy. He spoke and behaved almost as if he were interacting with another knight. None of the sharpness and disdain used with common soldiers had been evident. It seemed that being the lord's squire had a few benefits in addition to sleeping out of the rain. He finished brushing Wog with a smile on his face.

Alek went back to third rank's area to retrieve his bedroll and returned the old squire's belongings to the chuck wagon. He brought his shield with him. He figured it couldn't hurt to ask master Wayne about it. The little man took the shield from him and looked at it with appreciation.

"Yup," he said. "That's cowfolk work for sure. What do you want for it?"

"I don't want to sell it," Alek said. "I just want to know more about it."

"Well, I'm no expert," the wagoneer explained. "But I'll tell you what little I know. Cowfolk make the best shields out of leather. They are strong as steel, but much lighter. They are a lot easier to carry while marching, and they are expensive. One like this would probably cost 50 or 60 silver dots, easy."

"That much," Alek asked.

"Probably," Wayne answered. "I'm no expert, like I said."

Alek took the shield back, and looked at it with new interest. The front was painted with yellows, blues, and greens, depicting a cattle drive.

"Thank you," he told the older man, and turned toward the pavilion. A thought struck him suddenly.

"Master Wayne," he said, turning back. "How long have you been in Lord Bracken's service?"

"Thirty years, give or take. About fifteen with him and near the same with his father, why?"

"When was the last draft," Alek asked.

"Twelve or fifteen years ago, during the Bull War." The Bull War wasn't really a war. Queen Saffont, the queen at the time, had three cowfolk missionaries hanged for heresy. The cowfolk believe that every crime against them should be repaid. They call it, Eye for an Eye. So it was that every family member and friend of the three killed at the Queen's order, crossed the Big Sip, and killed one person in retaliation. Thousands of Murickan's were killed in a span of weeks. When the cowfolk met an army, they would kill one soldier, or die trying, then turn around and ride off. Luckily for the realm, the cowfolk who die avenging don't get avenged, or they would have just kept coming forever. In Alek's day, it was forbidden to touch a cowfolk missionary. They were uncommon, Alek had never seen one in real life, only heard stories.

"You don't remember anyone drafted from Brookville back then, do you?" Brookville was Alek's home town. He was thinking of his father.

"No, I'm sorry lad. I sure don't. That was about the time Lord Bracken took over for his father. It was a hectic time, and a lot of people died fighting the cowfolk."

"Alright, thanks," Alek said. He didn't find out exactly what he wanted to know, but he wasn't walking away empty handed either. There had been a draft when he was a baby. That meant his father probably had been conscripted into Lord Bracken's service.

Dusk was falling by the time he got back to the pavilion. He leaned his shield against the canvas of the large tent, and checked on Wog. The horse was as he had left him, munching some hay. He lay down on his bedroll, and all the day's events crashed in on him at once. His sore muscles protested, but it felt wonderful to be off of his feet.

"Hey," something nudged his foot, and he opened his eyes. Cholt stood over him, an angry look on his face.

"Yeah," Alek said questioningly.

"How does a dirtborn cowfucker like you get to be the lord's squire," his voice was dripping with spite.

"I don't know man," Alek said wearily. "Why don't you ask Lord Bracken?" His heart began to race and he mentaly readied himself for conflict. Cholt held no weapon, but his demeanor practically bled hostility.

Cholt said nothing in response, he just stood there, hands balled into fists, for several seconds, then abruptly turned and walked away. Alek would not shed a single tear if that guy died in the next battle.

Alek waited for his heart to stop racing, and laid his head back down. He would have a hard time getting to sleep after that. It crossed his mind to ask Lord Bracken for permission to sleep in the pavilion tonight, but what reason would he give? I *think* a guy *might* beat me up milord. Can I sleep with you tonight? He laughed aloud at the thought, and closed his eyes. It was a long time before sleep came.

It was dark when he woke up. He sat up, rubbing the sleep from his eyes, and looked around. At first glance, everything seemed normal. He started to lay back down when he noticed it. His shield was gone. Who the... But he knew who, he knew where, he just didn't know why, but that didn't matter. He put on his boots, got up and started toward the third rank area. His stomach was knotted with fear and frustration. He was nauseous with it.

They still had a fire burning, there were three men sitting around it. One of them was Cholt, and Alek's shield was sitting next to him.

Alek walked into the firelight and swung his fist, hard. He connected with Cholt's chin, knocking the bigger man off of the log he was sitting on. Cholt sprang up, cursing and ready to fight. Cholt waded in, swinging wildly. Alek stepped to the side and struck him twice more in the face. Hard knuckles to the face will scare most people and rattle their wits, Cholt included. He lowered his head and charged. Alek was helpless as the bigger man wrapped him in strong arms and took him to the ground. They scrabbled in the dirt for a few seconds, Cholt's comrades yelling encouragement to him.

Alek found himself on the bottom. He kept his head and shoulders moving, in an effort to keep his opponent from landing solid blows. Even so, he felt the jaring shock of impact several times. It was hard to see what was happening, with the dust and Cholt on top of him. He just kept squirming around until he got some leverage, and managed to flip the bigger man off of him. He stood up fast, but Cholt was on his feet before Alek could do any damage.

Alek threw his hands up into the larger man's face, who instinctively leaned back and threw his own hands up to protect his eyes. That is when Alek brought his right knee up into Cholt's groin. The bigger man bent over, clutching his balls and tried to say "Oooof," but what came out was a high pitched wheezing sound. Alek grabbed him by the back of the head and brought his knee up again, into Cholt's face. He heard and felt the man's nose crunch. It reminded Alek of celery being chewed. Cholt hit the ground like one of Wog's brown, tail apples.

Slowly, Alek turned and tottered over to the log where his shield was leaning. He sat down next to it, and looked at the other men around the fire. The fighting had awakened several more of the third rank, Tesson among them. He grabbed his shield and used it to lever himself back to his feet.

"I can't abide a thief," he said to no one in particular, and began to limp back to the pavilion. That was the funny thing about fighting. You didn't feel the injuries right away. How had he hurt his left elbow? His knee was the worst, and that was from Cholt's hard head. It felt as if Wog had kicked it. The punches he received were throbbing to life now. Several places on his shoulders and upper chest were sore to the touch.

People would think twice about stealing from him now though. They knew he would fight, and most of the time, that was all it took, or so his uncle had taught him. Stand up once, or back down for the rest of your life.

Chapter Five

A new day, a new boot. Alek woke up to the most pain he'd ever felt in his life. His knee was a throbbing mass, his left elbow was stove up, and both of his shoulders ached. He slowly opened his eyes and saw Lord Bracken standing over him.

"I heard that you had a rough night, so I let you sleep in, but it's time you got up."

Alek groaned as he rolled over and pushed himself to his feet.

"I'm sorry milord," he began, but Lord Bracken cut him off with a wave of his hand.

"Don't worry about it. I let you sleep in. Get Wog saddled." He turned to go back into the pavilion where his knights were gathering. He stopped abruptly, and said with a smile, "Nice shield."

Alek looked, and there it sat. The prize he had won twice now. He looked back up to say thank you, but the older man had disappeared into the tent. He got to work saddling Wog. His aches and pains lessened slightly with exercise. He was feeling better by the time Lord Bracken emerged to take the reins from him.

"Help Wayne with the pavilion and be careful with my maps," he said, then mounted the buckskin and rode off to the north.

As he gathered the hobbles and rolled up his belongings, he became aware that the camp was deserted. Everyone was gone. He was wondering how he was going to catch up, when master Wayne showed up. They got everything stored away, and the old man showed him how to carefully pack the lord's maps for travel. After they had everything loaded up, the wagoneer jumped up onto the clapboard seat and patted the empty place next to him. Alek climbed up more slowly, feeling every ache and pain.

"I don't have to walk," he asked with relief.

"Never," the old man replied. "You're the squire now. The squire *rides*," he said with a big goofy grin. Alek couldn't help but smile back.

After he got the horses moving with a couple of shakes of the reins, the old man scratched his gray beard and said, "I heard about your fight last night."

"Oh yeah," Alek said. He didn't know what else to say. He didn't want to brag about it, he had taken a beating too.

"Yup, it was the talk of the camp this morning. I heard that he stole something from you."

"Yeah, that shield I showed you yesterday," Alek said.

"Ahhhh, you got it back, I see."

Alek nodded.

Well, I doubt that anyone will steal from you again," the old man said and popped the reins once more.

It didn't take him long to figure out that he felt every bump in the road, with every injury he had sustained. It was torture. He prayed silently to the Weaver for a broken wheel or for a horse to die. Anything to make it stop. He would have gladly walked any distance, but he held his tongue and endured. Luckily the old wagoneer was full of stories and didn't expect Alek to talk much. They bounced along, the old man talking loudly over the squeaking wheels, and Alek gritting his teeth through the pain.

They caught up to the marching column just short of midday. Alek saw Cholt as he rode by, and he was suddenly thankful for the wagon ride. The man looked miserable. His face was one big bruise, and he practically drug his spear along. Wayne began to slow when they got to the front of the column. Lord Bracken saw them and called a halt. The old man stopped the wagon several yards ahead, and they prepared to hand out lunch.

Lord Bracken ate while Alek fed and watered Wog. This he actually enjoyed. He was much more comfortable with the animal, than he was socializing with people. Socializing was, to Alek, much like smithing. He could do it, and do it adequately, but he couldn't make himself like it. The funny thing was that he never actively tried to be a loner, it just seemed to work out that way, all on its own. Just like this. He didn't ask to be the squire, set apart from everyone else, feeding a horse while other people talked to each other, it just happened.

After all the men had rested, and filed past to get their rations, Lord Bracken took Wog back and mounted up. He looked down at Alek and said, "Are my maps safe?"

"Yes milord," Alek answered.

"Good," Lord Bracken said, and rode away. A man of few words, Alek appreciated that.

He stood there for a few moments, watching the nobleman grow smaller in the distance, wondering about his own future, when the wagoneer broke in on his thoughts.

"Levin," he said. "Let's get this stuff stowed away, and get back on the road.

They loaded up and once again began to bounce, squeal, and rattle down the road. Alek ate his lunch along the way. They passed the column right away this time, and went on ahead to find a good place to camp. Master Wayne explained that the clearing needed to be large enough for the whole company, the correct distance away, and near fresh water, if possible. The old man pointed out a couple of likely places along the way, but they were too close to the column.

"Lord Bracken will skin me alive if I burn up too much daylight," he said with a chuckle.

Finally, when the sun was in the correct position in the sky, they started looking in earnest. The first two likely spots were a little too small, and didn't have any water nearby.

"We can always backtrack a little ways if we need to," the wagoneer said.

A little further up the road, they found the ideal spot. It was a large opening in the trees that spanned both sides of the road. A small creek cut right through the middle of it and cut a shallow path across the dirt road. They decided to set up the pavilion in the shade of a large elm tree.

"Never set up under an oak," the old man advised. "There's a lot of acid in the leaves, and it will eat the canvas."

"Oh ok," Alek said, nodding. "That's good to know."

Not long after they finished setting up, Lord Bracken arrived and handed him the reins. He didn't waste time giving him commands again, so Alek had to assume that he wanted the horse untacked and fed. He retrieved the hobbles and the brush, after asking master Wayne where they were located. He finished his chores, ate his dinner, and drank the sweet clear water from the stream.

The evening passed uneventfully, and he was able to lie down, at long last. He decided to leave his halberd and shield in the wagon, with master Wayne's permission. He stretched his aching muscles, put his hands beneath his head, and closed his eyes.

His uncle's house was a burned husk. He could see the stars when he looked up. His mother and uncle were burned also. They both sat at the blackened remnants of the table he had been sitting at on the day he left. Their skin was charred black and flaked off when they moved. They both had large piles of blackened skin flakes at their feet.

"You left us," his mother said. "You're just like your father."

"I didn't want to leave, he protested. I didn't have a choice."

"You left us to burn," uncle Remi said. Alek watched a black spec of skin fall from his lip and add to the pile at his feet.

He turned to flee, but his aunt Tilda was standing in the doorway. Half of her face and hair burned away, the other half was disgustingly untouched. Her charred skin cracked and bled when she smiled. She held out her hands, and he saw that she was offering him a bloody child.

"Save her," she said. "You can do it. You can save her Alek."

"Save her," his mother echoed.

"Save her," said uncle Remi.

Alek screamed and ran, but there was nowhere to go. He tried to climb out over a wall, but when he looked up, the top of the wall stretched to the sky. He knelt in the corner and covered his eyes. In the way of dreams, somehow he knew it wasn't real, only the fear was real.

"Save her," all together now. "SAVE HER!!!"

He woke up with a start. He was shaking and sweating. It wasn't completely dark yet, so he had only slept for a few minutes. He took a few deep breaths and looked up at the starlit sky. The dream was already fading as he closed his eyes and drifted off, to sleep peacefully through the night.

Chapter Six

Alek awoke the next morning without prodding. He was sore, but feeling much better. It was still dark, but the first traces of dawn glimmered on the eastern horizon. He walked to the edge of the woods to relieve himself then checked on Wog, he found the horse resting with its head down. He gave the animal a pat and a scratch, then some soft kind words. He could hear Lord Bracken moving inside the pavilion, and saw a light blossom to life inside, so he moved to the front and stood by the opening, awaiting orders.

It wasn't long before the lord stepped through the flap and noticed him.

"Oh, you're awake already. Good," said Lord Bracken. "Fetch me some breakfast and gather my knights, including Sir Balto. He returned in the night with first rank."

"Yes milord," Alek said. "Should I saddle Wog too?"

"No, we will rest here today," the lord replied.

"Milord," Alek said, bobbed his head in acknowledgement and walked to the wagon.

With master Wayne's help, he located some good cheese and flaky bread. He took enough for himself as well, along with a few flakes of hay for Wog. He delivered the food and the hay, then started out across the camp to find the five knights. As he located them, he made an effort to remember their names. The five knights of Hardhome were Varn, Calemy, Balto, Raggo, and Wilton. Luckily none of them were sleeping, and they were fairly easy to locate in the morning light. When he was done, he removed the hobbles from Wog's front legs and took him to the stream to drink. The horse drank thirstily. Alek watched the big muscles in its neck move with each swallow. When he returned with the animal, he was able to overhear the conversation inside the pavilion.

"We'll stay put today," that was Lord Bracken's voice, "but we will be ready to move with a moment's notice. We are an equal distance from both bethels, if we move closer to one, it will put us farther away from the other."

He was answered with a chorus of "Aye my Lord," and "Yes my Lord."

Alek decided to get a stone from the stream and sharpen the blades on his halberd. This would allow him to do something productive while he awaited new orders. He found a stone that seemed acceptable to him and fetched his halberd from the wagon. He sat down near the tent opening and began to rub the stone along the ax blade's edge. There were a few things that he could do well. Sharpening a knife was one of them. He always had the sharpest knife in town. It was an odd, random thing to excel at, but he found comfort and satisfaction in the task. The stone made a soothing rrrriiiissssk, rrrriiiissssk, rrrriiiissssk sound as it moved along the steel blade. By the time he was finished, all three of the weapon's blades were sharp enough to shave a spider's ass. There was a small nick on one side of the spear head, but he did not think it would hamper the weapon's effectiveness.

The morning passed slowly. Alek sharpened most of the blades in the pavilion, all except Lord Bracken's sword. He wouldn't let anyone else touch it, and Alek didn't blame him. Just before midday, the lord came out to relieve himself. Before he could duck back inside, Alek spoke up.

"My Lord," he said.

"Yes," the older man said, his voice had an impatient edge.

"Do you remember anyone from Brookville during the Bull Wars milord," Alek asked.

"My first squire was… " he turned at the sound of pounding hooves.

"Milord," the out rider said as he reined his mount to a halt.

He was a thin man, clad in grays and greens to blend in with the forest. He wore a patch over one eye, and the thought of a one eyed scout struck Alek as funny. He was ludicrously tempted to say something to that effect, but thankfully the moment passed. The scout's horse was wet and winded, as if it had run hard.

"Out with it," Lord Bracken snapped.

The newcomer took a deep breath and said, "They are marching on Star Bethel milord. They will be there at midmorning tomorrow."

"How many," the lord asked.

"About a hundred. Mostly infantry, but they have the look of soldiers, or maybe guardsmen. They are professionals though, not farmers."

"Get something to eat and tend your mount," the earl said. He turned to Alek and said, "Fetch my knights," then disappeared into the pavilion.

Alek saw that four of the knights were already headed their way. He would only have to find Sir Raggo of the fourth rank. The man was probably shitting in the woods.

Luckily, Alek found him sleeping on his bedding. He woke the knight and relayed the order. Sir Raggo didn't respond, he just stumbled off toward the pavilion, yawning and wiping sleep from his eyes. Alek followed slowly, looking around for Tesson. He wanted to say hello and check on the other young man. They had never been close friends, but he still felt a connection to the other man, because they came from the same place. He didn't have any luck though, he couldn't find Tesson anywhere.

He got back to the pavilion in time to overhear the last part of the conversation voiced inside.

"Why not my Lord," it sounded like Varn.

"Because I want someone protecting our flank," the earl said. "Wilton will bear the standard. Everyone will go to sleep early, we march at midnight. That is all."

The knights filed out of the tent and headed toward their sections of camp, talking as they went. Alek heard them begin to shout orders to their men. The afternoon passed uneventfully. They ate, they rested. Rest was the most important thing. The entire company needed to rest before the long walk and fight to come. Alek laid down early, and was able to fall asleep right away, thank the Weaver. Lord Bracken woke him with a nudge, sometime later. The night was pitch black, the moon and stars hidden by the overcast sky. The only light came from inside the Pavilion.

"Get Wog saddled, and get ready to march," the earl said.

Alek got up without speaking, and went about his work. He worked slowly in what little light leaked from the tent. His stomach was in knots of fear and excitement. His mind took him back to his first battle and the exhilaration he felt afterward. He knew that killing another human being was wrong, he should feel bad about it, but he didn't. Was he a monster? He was a soldier though, and killing was his job. Did he really want to feel self loathing and regret for doing his job? Other thoughts filled his mind as well. They were fighting against the King's men. Why? Didn't that make them rebels or traitors? What about his father? He may have been close to getting an answer from Lord Bracken, but they had been interrupted by the scout. He wanted to get back to his mother to apologize, tell her that he loved her, and ask her about his father. He was a man now, he would sit her down and demand some answers.

As he led the horse to the front of the pavilion, he saw that the rest of the company was lining up. Lord Bracken took the reins from him and said, "Leave everything here except your spear and shield. Wayne won't be going with us, so you'll march in line with the other men."

"Yes milord," Alek said, and went to retrieve his gear. He rolled up his sleeping mat and put it inside the pavilion, in case it rained while he was gone. He got in line behind Tesson, just as the soldiers started moving. They filed past the wagon to get their morning rations, and ate on the move.

After he had eaten the last of his food Alek said, "How you doin' Tess?"

The other man turned his head and said, "I miss home. I miss my mom."

Alek couldn't see Tesson's expression, but his posture spoke of resignation. He walked like a man going to the gallows, and that might not be too far from the truth, Alek thought.

"Mar is dead," Tesson said.

"Yeah, I know," Alek said.

"You don't act like it. I know that you never had much use for us, but he was my friend, and I miss him. Now I'm going to die, fighting the King's men, and I don't even know why. Now that you're the Lord's *squire*, maybe you can tell me," he said, turning around and stopping abruptly.

Alek stopped before he ran into the other man, surprised by the heat in his voice. Someone bumped into Alek from behind and cursed. The column started moving around them, Alek ignored the looks and mumbles.

"Get back in line," Sir Calemy yelled, as he ran up to them. They did as instructed, and marched in silence for a time. Alek worried it over in his mind. Should he feel more for Mar? The three boys had played together as children, but had drifted apart as they grew older. Tesson had been right, he had no use for them. They both wanted to chase the cobbler's daughters and Alek felt like a fifth wheel. He was happy being alone though, he didn't need other people the way most did. He knew that one day he'd meet a woman to spend his life with, and that would be all company he needed.

"I don't know why we're fighting," Alek said finally. Tesson ignored him and kept walking. Alek had so many questions, and so much had been happening, that he didn't have time to get any answers. Tesson was right to be upset, they should know why they were fighting. Mar had given his life and hadn't known why. A man should die fighting for something he believed in. He did feel some sadness at the way Mar died, and for Mar's parents, they were good people.

The entire column marched through the darkness in silence. The loudest sounds were the clink of armor and the creak of leather. Each man was lost in his own thoughts, ranging from excitement to dread. They marched to victory or death, to which they did not know.

As dawn broke Alek saw the bethel in the distance. As they drew closer, a man gathering eggs at the chicken coop dropped his basket, and ran inside the stone building at the sight of them. Soon another man came out and ran up to the column, waving his arms in the air.

"We don't have her," he yelled. "Please leave us go! We haven't done anything wrong, we are true kingsfolk."

Lord Bracken rode up to the man and said, "We're not here to harm you or your folk good webinar. We are here to defend you. There is a company of kingsmen headed this way. Keep your people inside and clear of the fighting. Be prepared to flee, if the battle goes against us."

"Yes milord," the pious man said and turned to go back inside.

"Form up facing east," the earl told his men, and to Sir Varn, the closest knight to him, "Send scouts out to the north and south. I don't want them to get around behind us."

They lined up facing the rising sun, and began to wait. Sweaty palms clutched hardwood shafts. Soon a song broke the silence, low and smooth. It was a song that Alek had never heard before, a soldier's song.

He took the spear in misery,
He took the spear in pain,

He took the spear in chivalry,
He'd do it all again.
He was no knight,
He was no king,
He was no lordly man,
He took the spear to save her life,
And he'd do it all again.
We live to fight,
We live to die,
We protect the ones we love,
The Weaver spins us through the Web,
And we do it all again,
We do it all again.

The wait was so long that men had to leave formation to relieve themselves. Besides the singing, no one said a word. The span of time was thick with tension. Alek looked over at Tesson, and saw the fear writ plain on his face. His eyes were bloodshot, and the muscles in his jaws stood out, from clenching his teeth. He looked back at Alek and smiled without humor. Neither one of them said a word.

Eventually, the enemy company arrived from the east. They formed up across the road from Lord Bracken's troops. Again, the earl rode out to speak with the leader of the kingsmen. Both standard bearers followed their liege lords into the opening between the troops. This time Alek was close enough to hear the conversation, since he was in the middle of the column.

"Lord Bracken," the kingsman said, "I heard that you'd turned traitor, but I never would have believed it if I hadn't seen it with my own eyes." He was a big man, and stood ramrod straight in his saddle. His armor gleamed in the morning sun, unmarred by use in battle.

"I'm no traitor Elmund," Lord Bracken said. "I'm protecting my small folk and the faith. You don't have to do this. You can take your men to Lord Briss and help us do right."

"I'm a King's man, and I'm just following orders," Elmund said with disdain.

"It's going to be hard to follow orders from the grave," the earl said.

"In the name of the King, I order you to stand aside," the other man almost shouted. "I will do my duty."

"You're a butcher," said Lord Bracken, "and your duty is butchery. You won't face unarmed faithful today, by the Weaver. You will face the soldiers of Falcon Keep, and you will die."

Lord Bracken wheeled his horse around and took up position behind the line of spearmen. Wog wickered and pawed at the ground in anticipation of the action to come.

Alek hoped that his cowfolk shield was as good as they said. He was squeezing the handle so hard that his hand began to hurt. A bead of sweat ran into his eye, even though the weather was cool.

"Forward," Lord Bracken called, and was echoed by his knights.

Tesson made a whimpering moan and they began to move. The enemy line didn't charge them haphazardly as they did in the last battle. These men stayed in formation, shields up and spears out. Both sides picked up the pace, and started to jog. The two lines of men met with a crash and a chorus of shouts.

The impact jarred Alek, and he heard Tesson shout something unintelligible. This fight was completely different. The man directly opposite Alek, was trying to stab Tesson, while keeping Alek off balance with his shield. It was a mangled mess of sweat, blood, and shouts. Spear heads came in at Alek from different angles. It was all he could do to stay alive. A sharp blade grazed Alek's temple. He cursed and thrust with his spear. He felt some resistance, but couldn't tell if he'd hit flesh or armor. His shield held though, and he was thankful for that.

Cursing, sweating, and thrusting, Alek used all of his strength to hold the enemy back. At one point he felt something hit his leg, just above the ankle. He jerked his foot back and kept fighting. Was somebody stabbing at his feet? He grunted, jerked, and stabbed. A couple of times, his halberd was almost torn from his grasp. He learned quickly to make his thrusts fast. If he left his weapon out there too long, it would be taken from him. Then all at once, the man in front of him went down. Tesson, or someone else had killed him, and directly in front of Alek, about 5 paces away, was the enemy standard bearer. The bloodlust was on Alek, and he charged. The ragged cry that escaped his mouth was barely human.

Just before he got to the man, the standard bearer noticed him. The enemy turned and partially blocked the spear thrust. The sharp point of the halberd hit the man's breast plate and slid up over his right shoulder. The newly sharpened ax edge slid along the man's throat, opening the big artery hiding just beneath the skin. Blood fountained out of him, and Alek's momentum carried both of them to the ground.

Alek got his hands underneath him and started to move away from the blood, his hair was wet and sticky with it, when a spiked steel ball blasted into the ground, half an inch from his face. He rolled to his right and came up on one knee, in a fluid motion, and saw the enemy leader, Elmud, pulling his weapon back and wheeling around for another swing. Instinctively Alek thrust with his spear, taking the horse in the left shoulder. The animal reared in fear and pain. There was a heavy moment where horse and rider hung there, defying gravity, balanced. If the man would have released the reins he would have tumbled off, over the horse's tail, but he held on, and the large animal went over backwards. They hit the ground with a sickening crunch, as the pommel of the saddle stove the man's breastplate through his chest.

Alek was frozen for two heartbeats. Then he spun around to face an enemy that was surely coming for him. Instead, what he saw were enemy soldiers kneeling and surrendering up and down the line. He just stood there for a few moments, in a daze. His left temple and right leg began to hurt. He looked down and saw a bloody gash in the leg of his britches. Lord Bracken rode up and swung down from his horse.

"I'll be a web eating son of a camp follower," he exclaimed. "What on earth did you do?"

Alek looked around and took a step back, not sure if he was in some kind of trouble.

"I... uhhh..." he stumbled.

"You won the spinning battle, Weaver love you," the earl said, clapping hands on his shoulders. "I'll deal with these prisoners and let you see to your spoils. Make sure that they are both with the Weaver."

After making sure that both of the soldiers were dead, Alek inspected their gear. The breastplate had almost saved the standard bearer's life, but it looked too big. He didn't have anything else of interest. Elmund was a different matter. The armor he was wearing looked brand new, with the exception of the smashed breastplate. Alek removed the man's helmet and steel boots. These only made sense, considering the two wounds he had just taken. He also found a small pouch that jingled with silver. The real prize though, stood a few feet away munching on some grass. The horse was a good looking appaloosa mare. The wound he gave her had stopped bleeding, and flies were being attracted to it. Her skin twitched in a vain effort to ward them off.

He walked up to her, and grabbed the reins.

Chapter Seven

"She can't stay here any longer," brother Jensen said, shaking his head. "It's too dangerous."

"Well, what do you suggest I do," Mae asked? She had been on the run ever since the night she had taken the little girl away from the castle. She had assumed that they would be safe as soon as they made it to a bethel, but the King had proven to be more ruthless and evil than she had believed. The King's men had been moving away from the castle, burning and murdering the faithful every step of the way.

"I don't know," the old man said, shaking his head again. "You've got to get her to a high lord, one that doesn't wish to be king himself. Most of them would see her as one more obstacle between themselves and the throne. You can't trust anyone in line for the Murickan throne. Her safety is the most important thing though, and you saw what just happened outside. She isn't safe here. There will be more kingsmen, and anyone will give her up, after so long under the knife or the brand."

"Of course you're right," she said, running her hands through her short curly hair. Mae was one of the few female webinars in the realm. Most women did not want to give up the hopes of a family in order to serve the faith. When the High Webinar approached her with this task, she knew that it would be dangerous, but she hadn't thought about how difficult it could be. She looked over at the girl sleeping on the bench, and walked over to rearrange the cloak she was using as a blanket.

"You have taken on much responsibility," the man said. "You have the most important job in recent memory, and possibly in the history of the realm. Only time will tell."

"I am willing to do whatever it takes to keep her safe, I just don't know what that is right now," she said.

"The Weaver weaves us through the Web. You must trust in the Weaver. If you were not capable of keeping her safe, the Weaver would have chosen another. I have complete confidence in you. You are the most capable person I know. If anyone can get her to safety, it is you."

His praise made her feel a little better, but it could not erase the doubt completely.

"Thank you brother Jensen," she said with a wan smile. "May the Father guide me, I will do my best."

She walked back to the bench, picked up the sleeping girl, and moved to the door. She threw one last look over her shoulder, the room, brother Jensen, it wasn't much and she hadn't been there long, but it was shelter and people. Now she would be alone. She stepped through the door and moved off into the woods, as silent as a sunset.

From the other side of the building, she could hear the soldiers. They had just won a battle against the kingsmen. Thank the Weaver for that. If they hadn't arrived, or if they'd lost the battle, she would probably be dead now. She briefly considered going to them, but instantly discarded the idea. Even if she could trust them, too many people would see her, and people with the best of intentions talk.

It wasn't long before Carenia, (that's what they decided to call the princess, after her second favorite hero from the stories) woke up and was able to walk beside her. They followed the road, but stayed far enough away from it to conceal themselves from any passerby. She had a small knapsack on her back that she used to carry food. They stopped once to eat, but otherwise made good progress. They only saw a few travelers on the road, and easily evaded detection.

It was late afternoon when they came upon a wide section of the road with a small stream running through it. When they came to the stream, Mae searched around for the best place to cross, and saw a wagon and a large tent on the far side of the clearing. Between them, an old man sat at a fire cooking something. She made her decision all at once, and strode off into the clearing, the princes, or rather Carenia, in tow. Sister Mae had seen a few refugees on the road. They had been displaced by the fighting and sacking. She would use the kingsmen's search as her excuse for being on the road, and it wouldn't be too far from the truth.

As they picked their way across the little stream, the old man looked up and noticed them. Mae waved and he waved back. He stood as the companions neared the fire.

"The Weaver's blessings on you good master," Mae said, nodding her head in a polite bow.

"And on you good lady," the old man replied. He had green eyes and a gray beard, but wariness lined his kind face. "I'm called Wayne, I'm wagoneer to Lord Bracken. What brings you here goodmiss…" he trailed off expectantly.

"Mae, call me Mae, and this is Carenia," she said.

Wayne looked down at the girl, raising his bushy eyebrows and smiling. "It's a pleasure to meet you both. What puts you on the road during these perilous times?"

"The perilous times are the reason we travel," Mae said. Lord Bracken was a minor lord who could have no immediate designs on the throne. She needed to talk to him, but couldn't take the chance of doing so, while he was surrounded by soldiers. She knew that the lord and his men had been fighting to defend the princess and the faithful, but he was doing so on orders. Men would do almost anything if ordered to do so, no matter their feelings on the subject. Men in general, but soldiers especially, could justify almost any action when armored in the three words, "just following orders."

She *had* to have help though. She couldn't do this alone. Capable though she might be, she knew that one person alone couldn't accomplish much in this wide world, especially with all the strength of the throne set against them. She unconsciously squeezed the girl's hand a little tighter and told him everything, blurted it actually. She told her story in one long rush, barely pausing for breath. Later, she wouldn't be able to say exactly why she told him. Maybe it was the kindness in his eyes, or possibly she was just too tired and frightened to think clearly.

He just looked at her and nodded while she talked. He was already in defiance of the crown, an outlaw and rebel, so she supposed that one more step in that direction shouldn't frighten him much.

"You need to talk to Lord Bracken," he said. "He'll know what to do, and he's a good man, truly he is."

"Yes, I agree," she replied, "but I need to speak to him alone. I can't take *any* chances that he will hold us or deliver us to his liege lord."

"Aye," he agreed. "Lord Briss has his own reasons for opposing the crown in this, I suppose. I can let you spend the night in the wagon. It's a good distance from the rest of the camp, and I guess you must be tired. We'll have to be quick though, they should be back any minute now. Do your business in the woods and climb inside and keep quiet."

She did as instructed, fear and relief warring inside her. It wasn't easy to sleep, especially after the soldiers returned, but eventually she was able to drift off.

Chapter Eight

Anger stewed and bubbled inside Alek, as he marched along the road, watching the spotted rump of the appaloosa mare in the distance. Of course the earl should have the mare, he paid for the whole operation after all, but the knowledge didn't make Alek feel any better. He carried his helmet under his spear arm, it didn't fit just right, and it rubbed against the scalp wound. He would have to find some kind of padding to put inside it. Maybe master Wayne would have something.

He looked over at the line of prisoners marching next to their column. They had their hands bound behind their backs and wore a look of defeat. Alek huffed in irritation, and looked ahead once more. It seemed that his act of heroism had caused as many problems as it solved. They had no place for such a large number of prisoners, and no men to watch them. Lord Bracken's words came back to him.

"You did well Levin, and saved a lot of lives," the earl had said, "but now I have to feed all these men and find a place to keep them, and men to watch them. Nothing is ever as simple as it seems."

"But my horse," Alek began.

Lord Bracken cut him off. "The horse will pay to feed all of us, including *your* prisoners. If you can convince everyone to go a week without eating, I will gladly let you keep the horse."

The logic was clear and made too much sense for Alek to argue. He closed his mouth and went back to work tying up prisoners. At least he got to keep the silver. There were eleven pieces in the pouch, his lucky number, it seemed. As soon as he was able, he went to the well outside the bethel, to clean his wounds. Both of the cuts were shallow, but painful. It was said that webinars were the best healers in the realm, maybe the world, but they were shut up inside the building, hiding, he supposed. His wounds weren't that bad though, as long as he kept them clean, they should be ok. If they started to fester, he would deal with that when it happened.

As he marched, Alek went over the battle with his mind's eye, he relived it. He knew that he had done well, but he could have done better. He should have gotten a kill while he was in the shield wall. It was blind luck that allowed him to charge the standard bearer. What could he have done differently? The helm and the boots would help. It was difficult to make a decent offensive showing while you were worried about your own unprotected skull. Better armor would make him a better soldier.

His exploits had already made him somewhat of a celebrity among his peers. They had taken to calling him "Levin Bannerbreaker." He had always enjoyed the stories that he had heard while growing up, especially the ones about heroes with earned last names, like Ironheart, Crowbelly, Hardfist, and even Crag the Lustful. So, he couldn't help but feel a sparkle of pride at his new name. He wouldn't allow himself to become one of those boastful arrogant people that he disliked, but there was nothing wrong with feeling good about oneself, was there?

In any event, he began to carry himself a little straighter, and a hint of a swagger had crept into his gait. He wondered if his parents would be proud, if they knew. He hoped that his father might be, but he had a difficult time envisioning his mother displaying pride at the fact that he had killed two men. She was more apt to shed tears at the knowledge and pray to the Weaver begging forgiveness for her son. She had never been an overly pious woman, but neither was she a heathen. She prayed to the Mother, the Father, and the Weaver in equal measure.

She had been a great mother to him. Her only fault in raising him was that she could often be too lenient, in an attempt to make up for the loss of his father. He learned early on to take advantage of this, as any spoiled child would. As a rule, he had tried to be a good son though, never bringing her dishonor or real heartbreak, until the day he left that is. He still felt a mountain of guilt for cursing her that day. He knew that those careless words would haunt him until he received her forgiveness.

Maybe she could find another husband now that he was gone. He had overheard men in the village calling her a handsome woman. Alek hated the idea of her being alone in her old age. The weight of the coins in their pouch gave him an idea. Maybe he could build her a house one day. If his luck held through a few more battles, he could have enough. The idea lifted his spirits and made him forget about the horse that had *almost* been his.

When they arrived back at camp, Lord Bracken put Sir Calemy in charge of the captives. Alek drew the last watch, so he would not have to stand guard until tomorrow morning. He set about untacking Wog and the new mare. He asked master Wayne about another set of hobbles, and the man was kind enough to fetch them for him. He inspected the wound on the mare's shoulder, and felt a twinge of guilt. The wound seemed to be healing properly though, he was relieved to see. He fetched some water from the stream to clean the wound and applied some salve that the wagoneer had given him.

After checking with Lord Bracken to be sure that he wasn't needed for a bit, he went down stream a fair piece to clean himself up and tend his own wounds. He took his shield and halberd with him, the theft incident still fresh in his mind. The sun was getting low in the sky and he found a spot where the water looked inviting. He slipped out of his dirty clothes and put them on his shield, along with the pouch of silver. After inspecting his wounds as best he could, Alek walked into the water. It was cold, but not unbearably so. He sat down and rinsed the dried blood out of his hair, gingerly cleaning the wound in his scalp. It was painful, but the bleeding had stopped hours ago. He took his hand away and looked at it. There was a little fresh blood on his fingers, but not much.

The wound on his leg was about the same. It wasn't infected, but it was sore. He felt refreshed and clean, even invigorated by the cool water. He decided to clean his clothes while he was at it. He could sleep in his smallclothes and let the rest dry overnight. He couldn't get them completely clean. There were permanent stains from blood and sweat, but he was satisfied with the result. The thought of walking through the camp in his skivvies did not appeal to him, so he decided to put his britches back on until it was time to sleep.

It wasn't easy getting them on while they were wet, but he finally managed to get it done. He got his boots back on and bent over to pick up the rest of his gear, when he heard a commotion from the direction of camp. He picked up his halberd and started slowly in that direction, when an attractive woman and a little girl came crashing through the bushes toward him. They saw him, and stopped short, both of them gasping for breath, their eyes wide with fear.

"Please help us," the woman said.

"They were ambushed by kingsmen," she said, and again, "Please help us."

He ran past them to peer through the bushes the way that they had come. He saw kingsmen soldiers all over the camp. Instinctively he started back, he had to help them. Master Wayne, Lord Bracken, Tesson…

"There are too many of them," the woman said from behind him. "All you can do is die with them. We need your help, please." Her voice was thick with desperation.

Sometimes it was right to die with your comrades. Better a brave death beside your brothers in arms, than a life of cowardice. It didn't feel right though. These two obviously needed him. He looked back at them, saw the fear and desperation in the woman's eyes, but the girl just looked at him, calmly, serenely, as if he were about to serve her breakfast.

He went back to his gear and put on the wet shirt, tucked away the pouch of silver, and picked up his shield. He took one last look through the bushes, and saw nothing but kingsmen milling around.

"Ok, let's go," he said, and began walking. He had no idea where to go, or what to do, but he couldn't leave these two alone, to be butchered or worse by the kingsmen.

"Oh, thank the Weaver," the lady said. "The Mother bless you young man. You can't imagine how grateful we are!"

"What happened back there? How did you get here," he asked?

"Master Wayne was helping us. We were in the wagon, when we heard the fighting. We snuck away and ran through the woods."

"Master Wayne was helping you," he said, perplexed.

"Yes," she said, and drew a deep breath. The thought of telling someone else their secret so soon, made her queasy. "This is princess Delia, the true heir to the Murickan throne."

He stopped and turned. Surprised disbelief on his face.

"You're telling me that this is the girl that the kingsmen are hunting? She is the reason for all of this killing and fighting?"

"Yes," she said hesitantly, fear gripping her stomach in icy fingers.

"By the Mother's milk," he whispered under his breath. Then louder, "Where are you taking her?"

Sister Mae looked down at her feet. "Honestly," she said, "I have no idea. I have been wracking my brain, trying to figure out what to do. I have to keep her safe, that's all I'm sure of. My name is Mae, by the way. Sister Mae actually."

"You're a webinar," he asked incredulously.

"Yes, from Capital originally."

"I'm..." he paused for a moment, thinking. "I'm Levin, Levin Bannerbreaker," he said finally. He had earned that name, and he decided to keep it.

"I'm Carenia," said the little girl, "the warrior princess and protector of Florida!"

"We gave her that name to keep her safe," Mae explained. "It wouldn't do us any good if she were recognized."

"Oh ok," Levin said. "That is a spinner of a name. Carenia is one of my favorites."

"Yeah," said Delia, "she beat the three legged dragon, and made it safe for all of the old people. My grandma and grandpa are there with her now."

The girl was well spoken and intelligent for a nine year old. She would definitely have to keep her cloak hood up while they were around other people. That curly red hair would stand out like a torch at midnight. Almost everyone he knew, including himself and Mae, had brown or black hair, and usually straight, though Sister Mae's was curly. Curly hair was an uncommon trait in common folk, but not unheard of. Red or golden hair was a sign of noble or royal blood. Anyone who saw it would recognize her for being highborn, right off.

"Is it possible to change a person's hair color," Levin asked the sister.

"It is," she answered, "but it is difficult to do, and expensive. I've known some noble women who had it done."

"We should probably cut it off then, and tell people she's sick. We can't avoid all towns and villages forever. We'll have to take her around other people sooner or later," Levin said.

"We'll figure something out," Mae said. "You're right though, we are going to run into people, and it won't do to have her recognized."

They walked on in silence for a while, listening to the sounds of the forest. Chittering squirrels, clawing birds, and whispering wind played a natural melody that was balm for the soul. Eventually darkness set in earnest and they were forced to make camp. Levin found a likely spot, under a broad leafed tree. Levin rested his back against the trunk as the other two snuggled up together. They slept fitfully in the chill of the night, but they slept.

Chapter Nine

Levin woke up with a feeling that something was wrong. It was still dark, but moonlight stabbed through the trees giving him some visibility. He sat still, barely breathing, combing the woods with his eyes. He looked past a dark shadow, and was drawn back to it by what he thought was movement. He stared at it for two slow seconds, his heart beating wildly in his chest. It was movement, right there, and a shape congealed in the darkness. The form was large and canine, dark as soot, and moving slowly and silently, crouching in readiness to spring.

Levin jumped to his feet, shield and halberd in hand. He threw himself in front of the sleeping forms of Mae and Delia, as the wog lept. The large beast smashed into his shield, knocking him back a step and hit the ground snarling and snapping. He stabbed at it with his halberd, but the animal was fast. It dodged to the side and bit the spear tip, slicing its mouth in the process. The surprising pain enraged the beast further. It roared and snapped slinging bloody slobber in every direction.

The noise and commotion woke up the sleeping pair. They were crouched against a log behind Levin, he could hear Mae's frightened cries. The big animal, it was waist high to him, and probably weighed 180 pounds, began to circle to his left, dripping blood and saliva from its three inch fangs. Levin moved with the predator, keeping himself between it and its intended prey.

Without warning, the big canine leapt, roaring. Instead of raising his shield to block the attack, Levin turned toward the animal and thrust his with his halberd. The spear head slipped right under its chin and into the monster's throat. The animal's momentum carried it into Levin, ripping the spear from his hand and taking him to the ground. Once again he was doused in the enemy's blood. It was hot and pungent. He rolled the carcass away, and got to his knees. He looked at his two companions.

"Are you ok," he asked.

"Yes, we're fine," Mae answered. "Are *you* ok?"

"Yeah, I think so," he said.

The little girl got up and walked over to Levin. She stopped and looked at him with an intensity that he could feel. Those deep blue eyes boring into his soul. They stood there like that for two long heartbeats. Levin felt a chill run up his spine. Suddenly she blinked and turned to the dead wog, knelt beside the body, and started stroking its fur.

"She was just hungry," the little girl said, "and scared."

Levin pulled his weapon free, carefully, so as not to injure the girl.

"You were gonna be dinner," he said.

"Maybe," Delia answered, as she continued to pet the dead animal.

A feeling of dread and foreboding seeped into Levin. The thick smell of blood filled his nostrils and seemed to restrict his breathing. He felt slightly nauseous and light headed. He leaned against his spear and took a couple of deep breaths, trying to dispel the odor of death.

"By the Web," at the sound of Mae's voice, the tension cracked like thin ice on a pond, just before you go under. "What just happened? How did you know?"

"I just woke up with a feeling that something was wrong," Levin said. "That thing was creeping up on the two of you."

"Well, thank you," said sister Mae. "The Father guided us to you, I just know it." After a pause, she looked at him and said, "That's a strange shield. I'm no expert, but it doesn't look like metal, or even wood."

"It's a cowfolk shield," Levin said, holding it out for her inspection. "I won it in battle," he said, with just a hint of pride.

She took it from him, turned it over in her hands, marveling at how light it was, and inspecting the craftsmanship.

Handing it back to him she asked, "Is it, leather?"

"Yeah," he said, taking back the shield.

"Let's get moving," Mae said. "We need to get you cleaned up, and none of us want to sleep near that thing anyway." She motioned to the lifeless body of the wog. The princess rose and walked over to stand beside her. Sister Mae took the lead, picking her way through the gloom. They couldn't travel fast in the darkness, but they were able to cover some ground. The wog blood began to dry, and it made Levin itch irritably. He walked behind the little girl, and noticed that her red hair had a ghostly quality in the mottled moonlight shining through the trees.

Dawn was breaking by the time they found a stream. He washed himself thankfully, and watched as the blood dripped from his hands into the clear water of the stream. Mae noticed him checking his wounds.

"Let me see that," she said, not expecting any argument, and getting none. He turned his leg so that she could inspect the wound. She grabbed his leg, palmed some water over it, and scrubbed away some dirt, a little more roughly than he would have liked. He took in a sharp breath at her rubbing and prodding, but otherwise stayed silent. She did the same with the cut on his head, cleaning and inspecting it. She let him go and said, "They look good. No redness or swelling."

"Thank you," he said. He did feel a little better about the injuries, after having a webinar look at them.

They both sat down to rest for a spell. Levin cleaned his halberd, and found a rock in the stream to sharpen it. The axe blade was ok, but the spear had a few small nicks in it. He heard footsteps and people talking. He crouched down and motioned for the other two to do the same. The road was about 20 yards to the north, and a column of soldiers was passing by. Peeking through the bushes, he could see that they were kingsmen, probably hunting for Levin's little party. They sat quietly as the soldiers passed.

Levin noticed that the princess didn't look afraid, or concerned at all, really. She sat there with her hands on her lap, looking out into the woods, then at him. Then *she* gave *him* a reassuring smile, as if to say that everything was going to be ok. It shouldn't upset him that the little girl was not upset, but it did. He shouldn't be worried that the little girl wasn't worried, but he was. Something bothered him, it fluttered around just out of reach. If he could just seize it, turn it over in his mind's eye and examine it.

"They are gone," Mae said, interrupting his reverie. "Let's go." She got up, took the girl's hand, and started walking. They were going west toward the mountains, toward Brookville, his home.

"Have you decided where you're going," asked Levin.

Mae stopped and turned to look at him. "Yes, I believe that I have," she said. "I'm taking her to the cowfolk."

Chapter Ten

"What," Levin said. "Are you wrapped? There is a reason they won't cross the Big Sip, and it's the same reason we shouldn't."

"If I take her to any noble house in the realm, they will ransom her to the King, or... or worse." She didn't want to talk about certain things in front of the princess. "I have no choice. I have to trust in the Father, and do what I know is right."

Levin thought about this. She was right, of course. The whole of Murickan nobility, and most of the common folk for that matter, would see the princess as a means to an end. They would sell her back to the King, or kill her outright, but the cowfolk? He'd never met one in person, of course, but he'd heard plenty of stories. They were strange and dangerous people. Nomads and fierce warriors, they were constantly on the move, following the vast herds of wild cattle across the endless grass plains on the other side of the river called the Big Sip. Most of the stories told originated during the Bull Wars. The singers and bards loved to tell tales of cowfolk brutality and bloodlust.

"I don't know. I," he began.

"Do you have a better idea," the webinar interrupted. There was no animosity or sarcasm in her voice, she sounded almost hopeful, as if she wanted him to tell her a better way.

"No," he said. "No, I don't," his voice was tinged with resignation.

"Well," she said looking back at him over her shoulder, then she stopped and turned to him. "You don't have to come with us. I got into this situation with my eyes open. You had no idea what you were getting into when you decided to help us. I will understand if you decide not to go all the way."

He looked thoughtful for a moment, and said, "As you say, the Father guides us. I am where I am supposed to be. She is my rightful Queen, and I will see her to safety. I can't think of a better purpose for my life."

Mae heaved a sigh of relief. "Thank you," she said. "I was hoping you'd say that." She turned around and began walking again.

"I'm hungry," Delia said. "When are we going to eat?"

Mae looked over her shoulder at Levin again. "Soon," she said. She had left her knapsack in the wagon.

"Do you have any money," Levin asked her. "We are going back the way I came a few days ago. There is a village up ahead. If it's not full of kingsmen, one of us can buy some supplies."

"I have a little left, a few silver. I bought some supplies, but left them in master Wayne's wagon."

They arrived at the village around midday. They kept their distance and stayed out of sight. After talking over it, they decided that Mae would be the one to go. Levin showed obvious signs of recent battle, and his appearance might make people suspicious, or even scare them. She decided to walk around to the other side of the village, and enter it from the west, then leave to the east, so that she had the appearance of traveling the opposite way that they actually were. He nodded in appreciation of the idea, and handed her a couple of coins from his pouch. She was an intelligent woman.

After Mae had disappeared through the woods, he sat down and studied the princess. The little girl, she looked to be about 10 or 11 years old, sat quietly on a fallen log, her fine woolen dress dirty and torn in a few places. The cloak she wore was dark brown, and hid the dirt better than the light gray dress. She had a smear of mud, or something, across her right cheek. He saw the inside of a blood orange once, and that was the closest thing he could recall to the color of her hair. It was almost alive with color.

"Do you know why we're here," he asked finally. "Do you know what's going on?"

"Yeah," she said, looking up at him with those smart blue eyes. "My uncle's a wrapped nut who wants to get rid of me, so he can stay King."

Levin couldn't help but laugh, "Yep, that's pretty much it," he said. "We're going to do our best to keep you safe."

"I know," she said, matter of factly.

He argued with himself over the next question, but his curiosity got the better of him. "Aren't you afraid," he asked.

"No," she said. "You're going to succeed against him, but I'm going to be sad when you die."

Wait, what? "Succeed against who? Die?"

"The big man," she said.

"Who, the King?" he asked.

"No, my uncle is small and afraid. The Weaver weaves our lives and the Father guides us through the Web," she quoted from scripture.

"Succeed against *who*?" he asked again.

They both turned to the sound of bushes rustling and footsteps in the dry leaves. Mae had returned from the village. She carried a leather knapsack that bulged with goods.

She sat down beside Delia, and set the sack down on the ground, and handed Levin one of his coins. He looked at her quizzically.

"My father was a cheese monger," she said. "I learned how to barter before I was Carenia's age here," she jerked a thumb toward the princess.

"That's great, thank you," he said. His stomach rumbled at the thought of food.

The webinar reached into the bag and pulled out a wheel of cheese, a medium sized smoked ham, and a loaf of bread. Then she pulled out a carving knife and a chip of flint, and handed them to Levin, who immediately began cutting chunks of cheese and ham, passing them out.

"I also got some fishing line and a few hooks. We just need to find some bait, and we'll have fresh fish on the menu," Mae said.

They didn't have anything to drink and the food was dry. Levin and the princess both ate too fast and got the hiccups. Almost in unison, they covered their mouths, looked at each other, and busted out laughing.

Mae looked up from her food and said with good humor, "Keep your voices down children."

Levin looked at her, his brows pulled down in anger, "Who're you calling a child? She's not a child, she's a princess," he said, and laughed again.

"We need to get moving," Mae said soberly and began putting things back into the sack. "I'd like to have enough time to find a good campsite tonight. We can make a fire for warmth and to keep the wild things at bay, but we need to keep it hidden from the road. Kingsmen are as bad or worse than wogs."

Levin got to his feet, and brushed crumbs from his lap. It felt natural and right to follow the woman's orders. She was a natural leader, taking charge with competence and confidence, but no arrogance. He felt that they were going to make a great team.

They moved along the southern side of the road, several yards into the brush. They saw more refugees heading west today. The people who survived the kingsmen's wrath fled away from Capital. They moved along west in their twos and threes. Sometimes they had a wagon and a donkey, but most were afoot. It occured to Levin that they could step out onto the road and blend in with the crowd, but there was no sense in taking chances. They weren't under any pressure from time, and all it would take was for one person to see that red hair...

So, they made slow progress westward, and started looking for a campsite when the sun was still high in the sky. They found a good spot and got a fire going, just as darkness settled on the land like a mother hen sitting on her eggs. Levin went so far as to walk to the road and look back toward the camp. He felt satisfied when he couldn't see any light from the fire. Even so, he made a mental note to keep the fire small. When he returned Mae broke out the food again. She had gathered some water in a sheep gut bladder that she purchased, so no hiccups this time. After dinner, Levin went out to gather enough firewood to last through the night. He set the armload of wood on top of the pile, and laid down beside the fire, across from the other two people. It seemed as if Delia were already asleep. He stretched out his aching muscles, and closed his eyes, basking in the warmth of the fire.

"Thank you," Mae said.

He opened his eyes and turned to look at her. She had her elbow in the dirt, and her head propped up with the heel of her right hand.

"Aww," he said. "Don't worry about it. I don't mind fetching firewood."

"No, well that too, but thank you for everything. I don't know what I would have done without you." The firelight danced in her light brown eyes, turning her into something magical. He suddenly noticed how attractive she was. Nothing about her was too big or too small, everything was perfectly proportioned and spaced. She had emotion etched in her face, which added to her beauty, he just couldn't tell which emotion he saw there.

"Uhhh," he began. His face grew hot, so he scooted away from the fire a bit. "No problem. I would have done the same for anyone," which may or may not have been true, it was the first thing that came to his head, and fell out of his mouth like a wet rat. He wanted to take it back for some reason, but he didn't know why he wanted to do that. His mind was foggy and his heart raced. His tongue was coated in wool, dirty oily wool.

"Oh ok," she said, and laid down to look up at the sky. Was that disappointment he heard? "Well, thank you anyway. You saved our lives, and I can never repay you for that."

He kept his stupid, blundering mouth shut for a long time. Finally he said, "You're welcome." He almost whispered it, probably to no one. He thought that she may have fallen asleep. He had never been able to talk to women, not even to the cobbler's daughters back home. It was bad to even *think* about sex outside of marriage. Everyone knew that diseases were spread that way. The gods punished people who strayed, it was a wasting disease or one of madness, but they always ended in death.

Anyone found to be "sharing their roses," as his mother put it, could look forward to being ostracized and shunned.

It was common knowledge that the Age of Light ended in a time of madness, when the Weaver spun disease into the World Wide Web, to punish the wicked. Those who survived, did so by being monogamous and true. Knowing this did not stop his body from responding to a beautiful woman though, and his mind for that matter, even his mind betrayed him. To prove the point, his mind worked over their conversation at a fevered pitch, conducting a symphony of desire and humiliation.

It was a long time before he could get to sleep.

Chapter Eleven

The next morning was slightly uncomfortable for Alek. Mae was polite, but seemed a little cool to him. He figured that it was probably his imagination. He had little experience with people, and none with women. He berated himself for making up fancies. He had seen his reflection in standing water a few times, and once in old lady Thara's reflecting glass, when his mother had sent him over there to help her move her bed. It wasn't really glass though, just a polished piece of metal, and his reflection was hazy and a little distorted. He had seen enough to know that he wasn't the most handsome guy around, so the odds were that she wasn't interested in him that way, and he was just playing the fool. She was too smart and beautiful to be interested in someone like him, and she was a spinning *webinar* for Weaver's sake.

They had decided to go to his home village of Brookville. They would keep the visit short, and since it was his home, they could go in at dusk, when they were much less likely to be seen. The trip back home took a lot longer than the forced march away had taken. The slow journey gave Alek a lot of time to think. He went over his conversations with his mother and the more recent one with Mae. He seemed to have a great knack for saying the worst possible thing at the worst possible time.

It had been almost two weeks since he had talked to his mother. Had it only been two weeks? It seemed like a lifetime ago. He felt like a different person than the boy who had yelled at his mother. A different person, making the same mistakes with his mouth though, he thought agrilly He was looking forward to seeing her again, and the chance to apologize. As far back as he could remember, the two of them had lived with her brother Remi, and his wife Tilda. They had both been kind to Alek, and had treated him well. They were unable to have children of their own, so they welcomed the young mother and her infant son with open arms.

Uncle Remi had been the closest thing Alek ever had to a father. His uncle was a stern man, not very affectionate, but kind and fair. He made his living as a ferrier. He knew the blacksmith fairly well, and had asked a favor to get Alek hired on as an apprentice. He would have been disappointed at Alek's dismissal, if the young man hadn't been drafted, that is. In a small village like Brooksville, the draft would have been the hot topic of discussion for days, totally eclipsing his dismissal. He missed his uncle and his aunt though, and would be happy to see them again. He was sure that his uncle Remi would be interested in his battle stories.

At one point as they walked along, a fairly large troop of the King's soldiers passed them moving along the road to the west. This worried him a little, he knew that the soldiers would probably pass them again on their way back, and every time they passed, was a chance to be seen. He was right. Midmorning of the next day, the soldiers passed them going east. This bothered him, they were getting close to home. He pushed his companions to move faster. Mae seemed irritated with him, but he didn't want to explain it to her and give voice to his fears.

Soon, Alek began to smell smoke, or so he imagined. Fear quickened his steps and his pulse. By the time he broke through the trees above the village, the smell of smoke had strengthened, and so had his fear. He was almost in a panic now.

"Mom," he said quietly and began to jog. All thoughts of avoiding detection were scattered by the cold wind of fear.

He saw the smoke rising from several buildings. Some people hurried to and fro, others walked around dazed, or just stood still.

"Mom," he said as he began to run.

He turned a corner and saw his uncle's house. "Mom," he yelled as he dropped his spear and shield, and began to sprint. His lungs burned, "Mom," the big muscles in his thighs caught fire, "Mom," his stomach knotted and cramped. "Moooommmm," he screamed as a steady stream of hurt ran down his cheeks. The brave warrior was gone, the killer had vanished, he was just a boy again who wanted his mother, and all of a sudden, she was there. She appeared in the doorway of his uncle's house, with a perplexed look on her face.

He slowed, taking a couple of jerking steps, and fell to his knees. Relief flooded through him, but the fear and pain refused to leave immediately, and the tears continued to flow.

"Mom," he said again, weakly and thankfully.

"Alley," she said, and ran to his side, kneeling next to him. "Alley, is that you?"

"I thought," he began to say, but she wrapped him in her arms and began to gently rock him.

"Shhhh," she whispered, squeezing him tightly. "It's ok, I'm here. Momma's here, everything's ok." Tears began to run down her cheeks, but tears of joy and relief.

"Alley?"

He looked up to see his aunt Tilda coming from the doorway. She knelt beside them and hugged him too. Tears all around, tears for everyone.

His mother looked up at his companion's approach. Mae stood there, holding his halberd and shield awkwardly in one hand and Delia's small hand in the other. The three cryers untangled themselves and stood. Levin felt absurdly foolish, at being seen in this condition by Mae. His cheeks flushed hot as he made introductions.

"This is Mae and," he paused for a heartbeat, "and Carenia. This," he said, motioning to his mother, "is my Mother and my aunt Tilda."

"Call me Penny," said his mother. She held out a welcoming hand to his companions. "Please, come inside. I'm afraid you've caught us at a bad time." The entire group allowed Penny to guide them inside. Once through the door, Levin saw that part of the thatch roof had been burned away, and everything had been covered in soot, though his mother and aunt had been cleaning. In the corner laid his uncle, on a mat of straw.

"Alek?" his uncle asked. "Is that you?"

"Uncle Remi!" Levin said, and rushed over to him. "Are you ok?"

"Yeah, I think so. Those damned soldiers poked a few holes in me is all."

Levin looked up at Mae. "Can you help him?" he asked her.

"Let me see," she said, kneeling next to him and pulling back the blanket. His uncle Remi had three ugly wounds in his stomach. They weren't bleeding very badly at the moment, but they looked painful.

He stood and said to his mother and aunt, "She's a webinar." That was all that needed to be said. Everyone knew that webinars were the best healers. They stood silently and watched as Mae inspected his uncle's wounds.

"Thank the Weaver!" Tilda said. "Please help him!"

"I'll do my best," Mae assured her. "I need some webknot, powder if you can find it, but the whole root will do. I also need some clean water and some rags for bandages, also clean," she said in that competent commanding voice she had.

"I'll get it," Tilda said and went out the door.

His mother turned to him and said, "What's going on?"

"It's a long story," he said. "We need to talk."

They walked outside and found a quiet place to sit down. Levin was suddenly exhausted, as if all of his energy had been leached out of him at once. He told his story, as best he could. He struggled over telling her about the princess. In the end, he decided to tell her the truth. He told her about Lord Bracken, master Wayne, and the men he had killed. He told her about Cholt and his shield, about the wog and the ambush.

For some reason, he winced when she said, "Mother's love, Mae's almost my age. I couldn't imagine doing something like that. She must be a remarkable woman."

"She is," he said. He paused, knowing this was going to be hard for her, but he needed to know, "It's time you told me about my father."

His mother wrung her hands and looked down at them. She took a deep breath and closed her eyes. She stayed that way for a long time, and he began to think that she was going to refuse again. New tears ran down her cheeks, but he waited patiently, and finally she began to speak.

"Your father was the best man I have ever known, and the love of my life. He was drafted during the Bull Wars, to help defend against the cowfolk. Each cowman would kill one person, then go home. I was told that your father died saving a little girl on the other side of the mountains to the west. The cowman had reached back to stab the girl with one of those long knives, and your father put himself between them. He was unarmed. He sacrificed himself for a child he didn't know. I dream of meeting that girl and telling her about the wonderful man that saved her. I hope she's doing something grand with her life, so that his sacrifice meant something." She was crying freely and openly now. Forceful sobs punctuated every sentence.

"I'm so sorry," she said. "I should have told you sooner, but by the time you were old enough to understand, I had buried it down deep. I loved him so much."

He held her, and let her cry. It felt good to know his father's story. His heart was full of peace, pain, and pride for his father. My father was a good man, he thought.

"Mom," he said. "What was my father's name?"

"Levin," she sobbed. "His name was Levin."

Chapter Twelve

"By the *Weaver*," Levin said. "That's my name."

His mother looked at him with confusion, and he told her the story about how he got his new name. Her eyes widened as he spoke.

"I don't believe it," she said. "I mean, I believe you, but what a strange coincidence. The Weaver spins and the Father guides us through the web. I think that you are special son." They sat in silence for a few moments, thinking.

"I'm so sorry Mom," Levin said.

"For what?" she asked.

"For the thing I said on the day I was drafted," he said, lowering his eyes in shame.

"I don't know what you're talking about. I remember yelling at you for losing the job, but I don't remember what you said. I have been sick with regret since that day. I didn't want my last words to be yelling at you," Penny said.

"Oh mom, you were just trying to help, and get me to do the right thing," he said. "You did nothing wrong. I said something mean and spiteful, and I apologize. It has been bothering me this whole time, that I might not ever get the chance."

They hugged again, and forgave each other. They both held the embrace for a long time, because they knew that tomorrow isn't guaranteed. That realization makes one cherish those small moments with the people they love. Finally, they got up, and went back into the house to check on uncle Remi. The Tilda and Mae sat at the table talking, they both looked up as the two entered. Uncle Remi lay still, breathing the deep, even rhythm of sleep. Delia also lay sleeping, in a corner, on a makeshift bed of cloaks and clothes.

"How's uncle Remi," Levin asked the two seated at the table.

Tilda looked at Mae. "I think he's going to be ok," the webinar said.

"Thank the Mother," Penny said.

Levin let out a sigh of relief, and looked back and forth between his mother and his aunt. "What happened here?" he asked.

"The kingsmen came, looking for something," his mother said, and shot a glance at the sleeping child. "They never said what. They just turned the village upside down, put a spear in anyone who resisted, and left. They set a few fires, but didn't do much real damage to the buildings. They seemed to be in a hurry."

Levin nodded and looked at Mae. "I'm going to check the rest of the village, see if anyone needs help, and check for supplies."

"I'll go with you," Mae said. "I should see if anyone else needs healing."

"Ok," Levin said and turned to go. The webinar stood up and joined him.

As they walked Levin surveyed the damage done to the village, his home. The stone buildings were squat, strong, and well-made, but the thatch had been burned in some places, and was completely gone at the smithy. Stran Thatcher was working on it already. Old Bailer's donkey was tied at the hitching rail in front of the tavern. Not even an attack by the kingsmen could interrupt his daily drink, it seemed. They walked in silence for a short while. He wanted to check on the old lady Thara. She had always been kind to him, and had no living relatives.

"I'm glad that your family is ok," Mae said.

"Yeah, me too," he said. "Thank you for helping my uncle."

"I'm glad that I could help. The healing arts were the main reason I became a webinar," she said. "My mother died a long painful death, and I swore to myself that I would learn everything possible about healing. Death is the only real enemy, if you think about it. The kingsmen, and any other men, just do Death's work."

"You're right," he agreed. "I'm sorry to hear about your mother."

"It was a long time ago, but it still hurts when I let myself think about it. Thank you. I knew how you felt this morning, when you thought that something might have happened to your own mom," Mae said. "I'm glad she's ok."

"Thank you," he said, stopping in the road in front of Thara's house. The thatch looked to be in good condition. "How is your father?"

"He's doing well. He was a successful cheese monger. He has servants and lives in a big house by the sea."

Two women came running up to them.

"Alek, Alek," the both began talking over each other.

"Where's Mar," one said.

"How's Tesson," said the other.

Levin had a stricken look on his face as he shook his head and said, "I'm so sorry. Mar died in the first battle, and I don't know about Tesson. There was an ambush, he could still be alive."

Both of the women wailed in anguish. The one who had asked about Mar sat down in the road and began to sob into her hands.

"Where is Tesson?" the other one asked. "Where is my boy?"

"The last time I saw him was at a campsite a few days to the east," Levin said. "We were ambushed, and I haven't seen him since. I'm so sorry Maya."

They did their best to console and comfort the two women, but in the end, they just walked away. There was nothing else to be done.

Levin knocked loudly on Thara's door and waited. Levin looked back and saw the two women walking away, his heart sank for them, but there was nothing he could do. He'd always hated this part of going to Thara's. She couldn't hear very well. One time he had gotten worried and opened the door, only to find the old lady partially dressed. Her breasts hung flat like two empty wine skins. He could still see the way they moved when she turned toward him in surprise. After seeing who it was, she just chuckled and motioned for him to enter, as she finished pulling up her dress.

He dispelled the image with a shake of his head, and knocked again, louder. Nothing. Hesitantly, he pushed at the door, and met with some resistance. He looked down and saw some cloth on the floor. Whatever was stopping the door was wearing a dress. Levin forced himself to push a little harder. The door and the obstacle, now he was sure it was Miss Thara, moved. He was able to get his head through the door, and have a look inside. She lay on the floor, dried blood around a wound on her head, and on the floor.

"What is it?" Mae asked.

"She's dead," Levin replied in a flat voice, and walked around the house to find Thara's spade. It was where he had left it, the last time she needed his help. Silently, he began to dig a grave. Burning, unwanted tears burned his eyes. He didn't want to cry in front of Mae again. The shame made him angry and made the tears flow faster. He cut the earth violently, taking out his frustration and sorrow on the moist dirt. He silently cursed the Weaver at the injustice of it. How could you allow this, he thought. That kind old lady never hurt anyone, and now she was dead because she didn't move fast enough for some soldier, or because she said something he didn't like.

Thankfully, Mae said nothing. She didn't ask him to talk through his tears and his pain. She waited patiently, allowing her presence to be his comfort. Any more probably would have broken the fragile thing that he was, balanced there, neither boy nor man, but at the same time, both. Intuitively she knew to leave him alone, and he was thankful.

He went back to the door, and picked the old woman up in his arms, as a father would carry a baby. He recalled all of the kind words and sweet treats that she'd given him over the years. Tears fell on the dress that he'd caught her putting on that day, as he carried her to her new home.

He laid her gently down to rest and said the words that you say to the dead.

"May you be untangled, and the Weaver spin you anew.

May you know the Mother's love and live again.

The Father guide you to your next home in the Web.

You will be missed in this one."

He stood and forced himself to cover her with dirt. Throwing dirt on her face was the hardest part, she wouldn't be able to breathe. But she didn't need to breathe, did she? In truth, she wasn't there. She was being guided, by the Father, to her knew place. Was she being born on earth again right now? Or was she somewhere else, up in the stars?

He leaned the spade against the rough stone wall of the house and walked back to the road. *Why is this happening to me,* he thought. *I'm just a regular guy.* The heroes in the stories were all great strong men and women. They went on quests seeking vengeance and glory. There were no stories about fatherless, jobless, friendless 17 year olds. He was not ready for this. He feared failure, and failure meant people's deaths, not losing a job or a shield. Failure meant putting people in the ground and throwing dirt on their faces. He didn't think that he was ready, and probably never would be.

Chapter Thirteen

Mae followed Levin away from the grave. He walked silently, trying hard to keep his emotions contained. She looked over at him. His dark brown hair was straight and disheveled. He wasn't a big man, average height with muscular arms and legs. He wasn't a good looking man either, not by normal standards. His jaw was square, and he had beautiful intelligent eyes, but his nose was large, and his ears stuck out a little. No, it wasn't his physical appearance that attracted her so, it was everything else about him. He was courageous, kind, loyal, and strong. He loved his family, including it's adopted members, like the old woman they had just buried.

Every tear he shed for a loved one, drew her closer to him. He cared, really cared for other people, more than he cared for himself. That is how, for the first time in her life, she came to entertain the idea of breaking her vows. She had never really been tempted before. Oh, there had been better looking men who showed interest, but she loved her work and the faith far too much to be tempted. Levin was different. He made no attempt to seduce her, though he was clearly attracted to her, and that moral strength made him even more attractive. She was drawn to him like a moth to a flame, and she cared less and less if she were burned.

As they walked through the village, they found people who needed her help. She felt a childish pride at being able to display her skill in healing in front of Levin. Most of the wounds she found weren't life threatening, and one person was suffering from food poisoning, she was sure, though the man swore to the Father that he hadn't eaten anything strange. She put a pinch of soda powder in water, and had him drink it, then told him to rest. She would check in on him later.

Her proudest moment was at the trader's wagon. He had trundled in with his sturdy donkey at about mid afternoon. He was heading south on his return trip to Orange Keep, which could be named for the orange brick used in its construction, or the vast citrus groves in the area. The traders would come north with large loads of delicious oranges, tangerines, and grapefruits, and trade their way north, then return to do it all over again.

"I see you're coming from the west, how is it on the other side of the mountains?" Mae asked the tall thin man.

The trader pulled his hat off and rubbed his bald head. "They're all wrapped a little tight over there," he said conspiratorially. "The Bull Wars changed them, but it's no worse than it was last year."

When the socializing and news passing were complete, Mae got down to the business of haggling. She complimented the trader, insulted his wares, feigned insult and distress, in equal measure. The tall man seemed bored at first, but soon realized that he was bargaining with someone experienced in the craft. He actually seemed to relish the verbal dual, as he pretended to be wounded by her low offers and the deprecating descriptions of his goods. At last she pointed at the loaves of bread.

"How much for a loaf of bread," she asked.

"Eight copper each, or three for two silver," he said. Since a silver was worth ten coppers, you saved 4 coppers by buying three loaves at once.

"Eight?" she asked incredulously. "A loaf is one copper in Capital."

"We're not in Capital," he said. "Everything is cheaper there."

She picked one up and smelled it, "They are going stale. You'll have to throw them away soon. One copper is better than none."

"Five. I'll let it go for five," he said.

"I'll give you two coppers. That's double what it's worth, and you have already fleeced me for most of my money."

"Since you've bought so much already, I'll let you have it for three, but that's it," the trader said.

"Done," she said, handing him a piece of silver. "I'll take three." She waited with her outstretched hand for her one copper in change. The trader grumbled as he gave it to her, along with the three loaves of bread.

She turned to Levin, who was looking at her with those clear green eyes, and said, "Ready?"

"Yes," he said, and they turned to walk away. Levin had an armload of the items she had bought. "That was amazing. You got that bread for less than half of what he wanted for it."

"Thank you," she said, feeling a glow at the compliment. "As I told you, my father was a cheesemonger. He's old now, but he used to be the best haggler west of the mountains."

"I thought you were from Capital," Levin said.

"I am now," she replied, "but I was born in the west. I went to Capital to become a webinar. I haven't been west of the mountains in years."

"Well, you are an amazing haggler. I've never seen anything like it," Levin said looking at her with a smile.

"That trader was pretty good too," she admitted. "He got me on a few things. I am rusty."

Levin nodded and responded to people who greeted him on the way back to the house. He was aloof, but people seemed to genuinely like him nevertheless. They got back to the house, and Mae set to packing the goods into her knapsack, and the new one she had just purchased. Uncle Remi was still asleep, and Delia came over to help her. His mother got up and motioned for him to sit down in her place. He did so, and looked across the table at aunt Tilda. They both wore concerned looks on their faces. Mae listened as she packed.

"What do you plan on doing?" Penny asked.

The concerned looks turned to worry, and then fear, as he said, "We're going to take her to the cowfolk."

"*What*?" they both said in unison.

"You can't," said Penny.

"That's insane," from his aunt.

He could have said a thousand things right then, but Mae's heart swelled when he said, "I'm not leaving Mae to do this alone. It's the only thing we can do. We have been over and over it. It's the only thing that at least has a chance at being safe."

Penny began to cry. Mae felt pity for the woman, and guilt for dragging Levin into this mess. She stood up, walked over to the crying woman, and placed a reassuring hand on her shoulder.

"It's going to be ok," she said to the crying woman. "The Father guides us, and the," but she was cut off.

"It's *NOT* going to be ok," Penny screamed. "You're going to take him across the mountains to die, just like his father!" She buried her face in her hands and continued crying, but wracking sobs.

They heard Remi groan in the corner, then the little princess was there, kneeling in front of Levin's mother and placing her small hands on the crying woman's knees. Penny let her hands fall to her lap, and looked at the little girl.

"You will see him again," Delia said, "though, it won't be him, not really. You won't recognize him when you see him next, because the boy named Alek is dying, and there's nothing anyone can do to stop it. It will happen whether he goes or not." She looked at Levin, but continued talking to his mother, "A man named Levin will come back across the mountains." She said it so matter of factly, that everyone listening knew it to be true.

She stood up, went back to the satchel, and continued packing.

"By the Weaver," Tilda whispered.

"Ok," Penny said. "I get it. You're going to go, and I can't stop you, but you're not leaving without knowing how proud I am of you. You are the best son that any woman could ask for. I know what you're doing is right, and it makes me so happy to know that I brought such a man into this world. I will pray for you every day. Please, *please* be careful." She sniffled and wiped away tears, and Levin hugged her. He hugged her long and hard.

"I will come back to you mom," he said and squeezed her tightly.

Chapter Fourteen

Levin knew that he was doing the right thing by taking Delia to the cowfolk. Knowing didn't make it any easier though. He looked back toward the rising sun and waved to his family again. All three of them were standing at the doorway. Uncle Remi was supposed to stay in bed, but he grumbled so much that they let him get up to say goodbye.

"Alek isn't going off on some fool adventure without a good luck hug from his favorite uncle!" he had proclaimed.

Levin gave his uncle one of those butt-out hugs that you give to someone who is dirty, but he was just afraid of hurting his uncle's stomach wounds. He hugged his aunt next, she squeezed him tightly and cried against his neck. Lastly he hugged his momma, he held her for a long time, knowing that this was the last time he would see her for a while, and the painful memory of their last parting was still fresh in his mind. They said their farewells, made their promises, and shed their tears. Just as he was about to turn around, his mother stopped him. Reaching behind her she produced a short sword and scabbard, and handed it to him.

"This was your father's," she said. "Now it is yours. He may still be with us if he had taken it with him. I'm not going to let you make the same mistake."

He looked down at the sword, and scratched into the handle was the name Levin. Fresh tears bloomed in his eyes and blurred his vision. He hugged his mother again and thanked her. He wrapped the belt around his waist, and saw that one hole in the belt was worn from use. He smiled as he clasped the buckle through that hole and found that it fit him perfectly. The young man who had once been an apprentice blacksmith walked toward the western mountains bearing his father's sword and name.

They traveled faster this time. They kept to the road and kept Delia's hair hidden. Aunt Tilda had produced several small strands of material that they could use to tie back her hair. They remained wary though, and camped safely off of the road each night. On the first night, they camped by a creek, which allowed Levin the opportunity to find a stone and sharpen his weapons. His father's sword was well made, and perfectly balanced. He didn't know much about sword fighting, but he could remedy that.

He did know that fighting with a short sword and shield was different than dueling with a longsword. Real fighting wasn't the same as rodeo dueling. He had been to one rodeo in his life. His mother had taken him when he was 12 or 13. He had seen the knights dueling with longswords, and also the melee, where shields and other weapons were employed. Melee fighting was closer to real battle, where a person used their wits and awareness to stay alive, rather than skill at swordplay to please an audience.

The sword was already sharp, it didn't need much attention, so he spent most of the time just admiring it, and imagining his father. The blade was about two and a half feet long, perfectly straight, edged on both sides, and came to a point that was needle sharp. It could be used to cut or pierce with equal lethality.

"How are you feeling," Mae asked him.

"I'm doing ok," he said, switching his attention to her.

"I didn't ask you how you are doing," she said. "I asked you how you are feeling."

He looked at her for several moments, and she just looked back at him with caring and patience.

"I feel sad and guilty over leaving my family," he said finally. "I feel happiness and relief at finally knowing about my father."

"If Delia is right, you will see your family again," Mae said.

They both looked over at the sleeping girl. What if she *was* right? What did that mean? The princess hardly ever spoke, and when she did, it was usually to say something cryptic about the future. He looked back at Mae, the firelight flickered and danced across her light bronze skin. She continued to look at the princess for a long while.

"How do you feel?" he asked her.

"I'm afraid," she admitted, looking back at him. "In the beginning I thought that I would drop her off to someone more important than myself, and go back to my duties at the bethel. Not in my wildest dreams, did I think that I would be taking her to the cowfolk."

They both looked at the fire for a while. A million things could be said, but none of them should be said. It wouldn't do to complicate matters with either affection or rejection. Levin sighed and laid back, and looked up at the canopy of trees. Thanks to Mae, they had bedrolls now. He thought of her and his mother as he drifted off to sleep.

The trip over the mountains was thankfully uneventful. They heard the occasional mountain cat scream or wog howling in the distance, but their nightly fire kept them safe from wild animals. They knew, from traders and such, that there could be bandits in the mountains, but they saw none. The road through the mountains was well traveled, and fairly smooth, and they made good time traveling by day and sleeping at night. They discussed the option of buying donkeys once they crossed the mountains, horses were just too expensive, if they could even find one, but the idea of getting large animals across the big river was too daunting. They would travel the whole way on foot.

The first town they came to was probably two or three times larger than his home village of Brookville. The people on this side of the mountains were strange to Levin. Everyone carried a weapon of some kind, even the older children. Some carried home-made spears, the ends simply whittled to points, some wore swords across their backs, and some carried long knives tucked into their belts. Levin saw a woman walking down the street with a baby in one arm and a spear in the other hand. He pointed this out to Mae and she nodded.

"I heard about it from traders," she said. "It's because of the Bull Wars. After that, everyone started carrying weapons, just in case the cowfolk decide to come again."

The people looked strange to Levin. Their skin was darker than he was used to. They were the same coppery color as everyone back home, just a little darker. The women wore dresses, but the men wore knee length skirts instead of pants. The men wore their hair in topknots with the sides of their heads shaved, and the women wore their hair in long braids down their backs.

They stopped at a trader's wagon and asked about the nearest town on the Big Sip. The wagon was owned by a couple, and it was the woman they spoke to.

"Keep going west until you get to the river, then follow it north for a day and a half," she said. She took an animal skin from her wagon and held it out for their inspection. "Have a look at these furs, all the way from Ice Keep." The fur was dark brown, soft and supple. They begged off though, and continued on their way.

Levin felt guilty about taking up the woman's time and not buying anything from her, and said as much to Mae. She laughed and told him that the traders were used to people looking with no interest in buying. It was part of the trade.

Many days later, Levin lost count after four, they came to the river. All three of them stood there, looking at it in awe. It was so vast. Fishing boats in the middle of the river looked small in the distance. Levin had always thought that they could swim the river as a last resort, but that was out of the question. It was just too big. It would take the best part of a day to walk that distance. He was a decent swimmer, but he couldn't swim all day long.

They turned right and walked north along the bank. The topic of conversation was the unbelievable size of the river. The trader's stories had told them of a great river, but the words hadn't done it justice. None of them had seen the ocean either. They spoke of that, and how big it must be. They passed the time in the same way they had in the last several weeks, walking and talking. Their muscles were accustomed to travel now. In the late afternoon of the second day they reached the town that the trader had told them about.

The people were armed and dressed in much the same way as the other towns they had passed along the way. They went straight to the docks and began to look for passage across the river. The first boat captain only laughed at them and waved them away. The next one wasn't much better.

"Passage across," the captain said. "I was going to say that only wrapped nuts would want to cross the Sip, but I have known a few nuts, and none of them wanted to cross. They had enough sense to stay on this side of the river."

The third man told them of a fisherman that was down on his luck, and might do it for silver. They followed the man's instructions and found the fisherman bent over, cursing and muttering, while untangling some lines.

"Excuse me," Levin said.

The man looked up, obviously irritated by the interruption.

"What do you want?" he said.

"We want passage across the river, and we can pay," Mae said.

"Why on the Web would you want to cross?" the man asked.

"That's our business," Mae said. "Do you want to make some money, or not?"

The man was silent for a few moments. He looked at the rope in his hands, and sighed.

"One silver for each of you," he said finally.

"Two silver for all of us," Mae replied.

"Three silver, or go find someone else," he said with finality.

Mae looked at Levin and he shrugged. They didn't know if they would even need silver on the other side.

"We'll pay you on the other side," she said with equal finality.

"Ok, get in," the fisherman said as he began to untie his boat.

They did as directed, and found places to sit that were fairly stable. It wasn't a small boat, they had room to move around. The man pushed the boat away from the dock and raised the sails, whistling as he worked. Levin scratched at his new beard. He was going to shave it, but Mae had made a remark about how much she liked it, so he left it alone.

The crossing took about an hour. After paying the man, they had to jump out into waist deep water because there weren't any docks on the western side of the river. Once they were safely on the western shore they looked back across the river, and then at each other. Unspoken words hanging in the air.

There was no going back. They were in cowfolk country now.

Chapter Fifteen

After discussing it, they struck out due west across the plains. There were no roads to follow or landmarks to go by. The ground was flat and covered in ankle deep grass as far as the eye could see. When Levin turned to look back across the river, it seemed like a different world over there, with the mountains in the distance, and the variations in color.

As they walked they talked about everything. Talking was the only way to pass the time. They had learned weeks ago that walking quietly was not fun. The monotony of silence could drive a person crazy. So they talked and shared their lives, hopes, and dreams with each other.

Levin told them about the time he found a baby owl with a broken wing. He took it home with him and made a little splint for its wing. He fed it meat from his own plate, and cared for it all winter. He couldn't tell whether it was male or female, so he named it Nightwing. Uncle Remi bought him a pair of leather gloves from a trader's wagon, to protect his hands from the sharp little claws and beak. He grew very fond of the little raptor, but one day, without warning, it just flew away, and he never saw Nightwing again. It was a bitter-sweet memory for Levin. The young bird would have certainly fallen prey to another creature, or starved to death without his intervention. He watched the sky for months afterward, hoping that Nightwing would return.

Mae looked at him oddly as he told his story, was that pity? He instantly regretted telling her. He did not want her to see him as a pitiful child. He knew that he would never get to marry her, but he still couldn't help trying to be better for her. He was afraid of doing or saying anything that would lower her opinion of him. Without realizing it, she was already making him a better man.

At one point they saw a pride of lions in the distance. The big cats looked at them without interest. The huge male yawned and its large fangs were visible at a distance, bright in the sunlight. After that, they kept their eyes open, and kept their distance. They knew that the cowfolk followed huge herds of cattle, so it made sense that there would be some big predators who preyed on the cattle as well.

The small group spent the night in some ancient ruins. Levin stared, awestruck, at one of the structures. It was easily the tallest thing he had ever seen, not counting the mountains. It had to be ten times taller than any tree. Levin had a hard time imagining that people could build anything as monumental as that, and said as much to Mae.

"In our learning at the Rose Bethel, we are taught about the Age of Information," she said. "It is said that people could fly, talk to each other from anywhere in the world, build to the sky and cross oceans."

He looked at her in frank disbelief.

"People could access the World Wide Web to learn and do just about anything," she went on. "But, the humans were full of pride and refused to follow the Father's guidance, so the Weaver wove a great plague into the web. The emps stole their power, and sent them back to the Stone Age. The people were in love with hatred and war. They were like this king we have now. If we don't stop him and put the rightful heir on the throne, I'm afraid that the emps will return and steal our fire or worse."

"Is that where emps came from? I have heard people talk about them, but I always thought that they were like wogs or something," Levin said.

"Yes it is," Mae answered. "The emps were sent by the weaver to steal our power. They are dark creatures that feed on light and knowledge. They are the Weaver's tools to set things right on earth, and if they come again, we will be left as animals. Can you imagine life without fire or metal?" She shuddered at the thought.

"And the webinars protect us from them?" Levin asked, very interested now.

"Our main duty is to keep knowledge alive. Everything that we know belongs to us. We can't allow a king to have it taken away. The human race is good, but individual people can be evil, and when they gain power, that evil can spread like a disease. Power corrupts, not just the ruler, but the entire kingdom," Mae said.

"So, what we are doing goes far beyond saving one little girl," Levin said thoughtfully.

"Exactly," Mae answered. "It's up to all of us to keep our realm safe, and the webinars will always be here to make sure that we do."

Levin was deep in thought as he went out to find fuel for the fire. There were no trees on the plains, so therefore no wood, but he did find some old cow patties. They were dry, odorless, and abundant. They made camp in the shadow of the prehistoric monolith.

Levin looked at Mae as he sat down beside the fire. She was watching the little girl, who was already asleep. Keeping his voice barely above a whisper he said, "Everything alright?"

"Hmm?" Mae said, turning to look at him.

"I asked if everything's ok," Levin said.

"Oh, yeah," Mae said. "I was just thinking. Delia was an average little girl when I first met her a few weeks ago, but she has changed somehow."

"What do you mean?" Levin asked, looking over at the sleeping girl.

"She's not as talkative, quieter, and... mature. It's almost like she's a different person, or like she's grown up all at once."

"Well, she's been through a lot," Levin said. "Maybe she'll return to normal after we get her to a safe place and she gets settled down."

"You're probably right," Mae said. "I'm just worried that she will lose her childhood. She should be playing and laughing, not running for her life and worrying about the kingdom."

Levin nodded thoughtfully. "The Father guides us right?" he asked.

"Yes," Mae answered with a smile. "The Father guides us, and I know that what we're doing is right. I just worry about her."

"Everything's going to be ok," Levin said, and laid his head down to get some sleep.

He dreamed that he was caught in a large web. Chittering green emps, crept toward him, venom dripping from their fangs. He struggled to escape, opened his mouth to scream, but no sound came out. He knew intuitively that if those emps touched him with their too human hands, he would go mad. They got close enough that he could smell their rotten breath, and see his reflection in their eyes, like looking into old lady Thara's mirror, distorted and hazy.

He sat bolt upright, breathing heavily and looking around. The dream was still fresh in his mind. He threw more fuel on the fading fire, and lay back down. He looked at the stars for a few minutes, they were so bright out here. He slowly became aware of the feeling that he was being watched. He sat up again, and peered into the darkness. Probably an animal, he supposed, padding around in the darkness, afraid of the fire. He threw more fuel on the fire, just to be safe, and lay down again. Sleep did not come quickly.

"You plan on sleeping all day?" Mae asked, giving him another shake.

"Huh," Levin said, shaking his head, and raising his hand to block the morning sunlight.

"Time to get moving," Mae said as she packed her knapsack.

Levin struggled to his feet and walked over near the large structure to relieve himself. He looked down and saw a human footprint in the soft ground.

"Mae, come here!" he called.

She looked over at him and said, "I'm not looking at that until after we're married."

"No, not that," he said, looking down at himself and tucking his manhood back inside his pants. "Come here and look at this track!" *After* we're married?

She did as he asked, and studied the print for several seconds. She squatted down beside it for a better look.

"Well," she said finally. "It looks like they know we're here, and they haven't killed us. That's good news, if I've ever heard any."

"Yeah, I guess you're right," Levin said. "It just makes me a little nervous to think of them watching us sleep."

"Not much we can do about it," she said over her shoulder as she walked back to the fire. "They are fierce when provoked, but I've never heard any stories about them attacking without cause. Have you?"

"No," he said reluctantly. "No I haven't, but,"

"But we're alive. That's what matters," Mae said, cutting him off.

They finished packing up, Mae helped Delia get her things back in her sack. The party, once again, faced away from the rising sun, and set off. It was about midmorning when they came across a gigantic path cut into the grass by cattle hooves. Like the river, the immensity of it staggered the mind. It was difficult to guess, but it had to be at least a mile across. Levin tried to imagine the number of cattle it would take to eat and walk that much grass down to the dirt, and he couldn't. He could only come up with, "millions," which could be way off.

They followed the awesome trail for several hours, and found a stream with old campfires on either side of it. The water was clear and cool. Mae said a quick prayer to the Mother and topped off their canteens. Levin inspected the abandoned camp as she did so. He saw many human prints, large and small, what looked like cow bones, and some animal prints he thought probably belonged to dogs.

They continued to follow the unbelievably massive trail for the rest of the day. Every so often they would come across signs of humanity, a scrap of cloth or leather, a cooked bone, and more small toilet holes than they cared to count. They knew what the little holes were for because of the little grass mats that accompanied them. Every little mat had a brown smear of feces on it. Levin actually picked up the first one they found and gave it a sniff. Mae and Delia had both laughed when he told them what they smelled like. He chased Delia with the smelly mat as she squealed in terror.

Other than the poop incident, which Mae had begun to call it, with a giggle every time she said it, the day passed uneventfully. They camped again with a fire made of cow manure. Mae said that it was right for Levin to gather the fuel for their fire, since he was the expert. She giggled at her own hilarity as he stomped off good naturedly.

When he returned, he dropped the armload of patties next to the fire, and sat down on his bedding. Delia was sleeping and Mae was lying down staring up at the sky.

"Are you ok?" he asked Mae quietly.

"Hmmm? Oh yeah, I'm fine," she said. "I was just thinking."

"About what?" he asked.

"Everything," she said. "Everything that we're leaving behind. I have spent my entire adult life as a webinar, and giving that up isn't easy. I wonder if I can go back to the Webinary, or have I sacrificed everything forever."

"What's a Webinary?" Levin asked. He hadn't really thought about how much she'd given up for this. He felt a bitter prick of self disgust. What had he been worried about? What was he leaving behind? Thinking about all that Mae was sacrificing made his worries tiny by comparison.

"It's the order I belong to. We are called webinars, because we belong to the Webinary, as do the bethels," Mae said.

"The Webinary will miss you," Levin said. "I wish there was something I could do," he trailed off. Levin hated feeling helpless, and he hated problems that had no solution.

"Thank you," Mae said, looking over at him. "I'm glad you came."

"You are doing a good thing, the right thing," Levin said. Looking at her now, it struck him again how beautiful she was, even travel weary and in the light of a dung fire. Just by looking at him, she made his pulse race and set his cheeks aflame. "I'm glad I came too."

"Goodnight Levin Pattybreaker," Mae said laughing, and rolled over on her side.

Levin fell asleep with a smile on his face, in spite of, and more likely because of, the ribbing he had taken. He slept peacefully on their second night in the plains.

Chapter Sixteen

It was the morning of the fifth day before they saw smoke trails on the horizon, denoting many campfires, and many more hours of walking before they saw any actual sign of human habitation. They topped a large sloping hill, and down below them was the largest group of people Levin had ever seen. Tents stretched to the horizon. There were *hundreds* of horses staked out around the outside of the vast camp, grazing. Levin had not known that there were so many horses in existence. He stared at the sight for several seconds, disbelieving. Was everything gargantuan on this side of the Big Sip? The numbers were staggering.

Their journey complete, there was nothing to do but go down there. They rose slowly, and started toward the camp. When they were about half way down the hill, they saw commotion in the camp, and a dozen people armed with bows and spears rode up and surrounded them. They raised their hands in the universal sign of peace. Delia stood close to Levin, as if for protection.

"Watcha' doin'ere," the speaker was a muscular man, holding a horn bow with a nocked arrow pointed at Levin's chest. His speech was strange, and difficult to understand, as if the words were being mashed together.

"My name is Levin Bannerbreaker," Levin said. "We have come to ask for shelter for this little girl," he nodded to Delia. "People across the river are trying to kill her."

The man who had spoken grunted and jerked his head to one of his companions, who dismounted and began to tie their hands behind their backs, with leather thongs. Levin's weapons and shield were taken from him. He didn't like this at all. They were all very personal possessions, and he cherished each of them for a different reason. He said as much, but only got another grunt in reply.

The small party was made to walk to camp, trailed closely by the dozen riders. Mae had a worried look on her face, but Delia was stoic, as usual.

The gaps between the staked horses was much larger than it had seemed from a distance. The entire group walked into camp and was met by a smaller one. The leader of this group was an average sized man of about 40 years. He wore his long brown hair in two braids down his back. He was clad, as all of the people were, in a buckskin shirt and pants. His clothing was dyed a mottled green and tan pattern that would make him virtually disappear out in the grass. He had a calm commanding demeanor, and light skin. All of them had light skin.

"I'm William," he said, in the same strange way that the first man had spoken, "Gobnor ofthe StoneSnakes. Why're ya'here?"

"I am Levin, this is Mae and Delia. People in the east want to kill the little girl," Levin said. "We brought her here hoping to keep her safe."

The man looked down at Delia, then at Mae, and back at Levin. His sharp eyes missed nothing. Levin felt weighed and measured with that quick glance.

"Bring'em," William said, spun on his heel, and started walking into camp. Levin followed with a shove from behind.

As they wove their way through the tents, Levin heard shouts and screams in the distance. William stopped the group to listen for a moment, and turned to the man who had spoken on the hill.

"Sam," he said. "Take them to my tent and watch them." He turned and ran toward the sounds.

Sam, guided them quickly to a large tent, shoved them inside, and posted himself as guard outside the entrance.

"What's going on," Mae asked.

Levin ignored the question and began to search the tent. The sounds, now obvious sounds of battle, were growing closer. He found a square ornate box of polished wood, with gold inlay, and kicked it over.

"What are you doing," Mae asked.

"Looking for a way to cut these bonds," Levin said as he toed the lid open. He found what he was looking for, a small axe. It was an ornate, one handed weapon, more of a hatchet really. He knelt down and tried to position the blade in a way that he could cut the leather thong that bound his wrists. It wasn't easy, but he finally managed to get it done. He stood up holding the axe, when two people burst into the tent, a small woman and child. They ran to the back of the tent and huddled against the wall in fear. He looked at Mae and Delia, who were both wide eyed with fear, and motioned for them to get behind him.

There was a commotion outside the tent flap, and Sam the guard, fell backward through the opening with a knife buried in his chest. A woman came in behind him and bent down to retrieve her knife. Levin took two steps and swung the axe hard. The stranger didn't have much time to react. She threw her left arm up to ward off the blow. Levin's axe took her in the forearm, almost severing it. He felt a sharp click as the blade snapped the bone.

The enemy let out a visceral scream and swung the knife at Levin, who caught the woman's wrist in his free hand. He brought the axe down again, where the neck meets the shoulder, cleaving through collar bone and rib. The attacker fell, spurting blood from two savage wounds, and died at his feet. He picked up the knife, cut Mae's bonds, and gave it to her, then motioned for her to take Delia to the back of the tent with the other two.

He took up position at the doorway, ready to ambush anyone who came through. Bloodlust surged through his veins. He almost hoped that another enemy came through the opening. Then his eyes dropped to the woman he had killed and the desire faded. He said a silent prayer to the Weaver for the two dead people in the doorway. The battle sounds raged on outside, but after a long while, it settled down. He heard someone coming to the entrance. He assumed that it was someone friendly, but he readied himself for action just in case. The newcomer paused at the entrance, as if surveying the dead bodies, and finally parted the tent flaps cautiously.

William peered through the entrance. The cowfolk woman and child jumped up and ran to him, and hugged him tightly. He looked at Levin, then down at the axe he held.

"Holy Mother," he said. He guided his wife and child outside and looked at Levin. "Stay'ere. Don't move," and he left.

Levin checked on Mae and Delia. Delia's wrists were free, and both were unharmed.

"What do you think he went to do?" Mae asked.

"I have no idea," Levin said. "He can't be too upset with me. I saved his wife and son." The trio waited, asking nervous questions that no one could answer, and not looking at the dead bodies in the doorway. Finally after about an hour, William returned.

"You," he pointed at Levin, "comewit'me."

Levin followed him with a glance back at Mae that was supposed to be reassuring. He still carried the axe, he wasn't going to release it unless someone told him to. They walked until they came to a very large tent. William ducked inside, and Levin followed. As soon as he stood up straight, people started yelling and waving their hands. There were about 20 people seated on the floor of the tent, every one of them older than 40, and some looked over 60.

William raised his hands for quiet, but the shouting continued.

"Why's he untied?"

"He's got Snakeclaw!"

"Why's hegot our sacredaxe?"

"What thehell's goingon?"

William waited patiently for the noise to subside. At last it was quiet enough for him to speak without yelling.

"This man calls himself Levin Bannerbreaker," he said. Levin was having an easier time understanding them now. The more he listened, the easier it became. "He slew an enemy during the raid. He defended the camp, and he used Snakeclaw to do it."

There was an immediate uproar. William nodded, as if expecting this, and raised his hands again. This time he didn't wait for the noise to die down. He raised his voice above the din.

"Our laws are clear. He saved my wife and son with Snakeclaw, and he did it defending this camp during a raid."

The noise died down slowly as people began to talk and whisper to each other individually.

"What does all this mean?" Levin asked.

William turned to him with a smile and said, "It means thank you for protecting my family, especially when you were a prisoner. It means that you are a member of our clan, as if you were born here, and it means that the axe, Snakeclaw, belongs to you. It is sacred to us, so I hope you will return it to its rightful place once I've returned your weapons to you."

Chapter Seventeen

On their way back to his tent, William continued to explain.

"It is our law that any slave who defends the clan during an attack, wins there freedom and becomes a brother or sister of the clan," he said

"Slave?" Levin said.

"Yes," William said matter of factly, as if he were discussing saddling a horse. "You and the little girl belonged to me. You earned your place among us by defending the camp, and I give you the girl for defending my family."

"We do this," William continued his first line of thought, "to protect the slaves. A person cannot order their property to take up arms and defend the clan in their stead, without consequences. The slave forced to fight in the owner's place can take revenge with the weapon they used to defend the owner.

Levin walked along only half listening. He decided that he didn't like the backward savages who had killed his father. Slaves? He could not be owned. The thought of it curdled his stomach. A person was born free to travel the Web and forge their own destiny. The notion of slavery irritated him even more because he had so narrowly escaped it.

When they arrived back at William's tent, Levin saw his belongings leaning up against it. He handed the axe to William, who ducked inside, and strapped on his sword belt. Picking up his shield and halberd, he ducked inside as well.

He saw Delia sitting there in that quiet way she had, opened his mouth to ask Mae how everything went while he was gone. He couldn't find her. She wasn't there where he'd left her.

"Where's Mae," he asked William.

"The woman?" William asked.

"Yes, the spinning woman. The woman I left here a little while ago. The woman I came with," Levin said, getting irritated.

"As I told you," William said. "You and the girl belonged to me, but not the woman. She belongs to Joseph. I suppose he came and got her."

"What?" Levin almost shouted, and dashed out through the opening, screaming her name. "Mae!"

He took off running in a random direction, knowing it could be the wrong way, but not caring. His heart beat wildly, his muscular legs ate distance rapidly.

"Mae!"

"Levin," in the distance, he couldn't tell which direction. He stopped.

"Mae!" he yelled again, his voice getting hoarse.

"Levin," to the left he ran, in the direction of her voice.

"Levin," he heard again, closer, much closer.

Then he saw her, being led by the largest man Levin had ever seen. He had her by the upper arm, and they both turned at the sound of Levin's voice.

"Stop," Levin yelled with as much authority as he could muster with his hoarse voice. "She belongs to me."

As the man turned, Levin began to feel ill. So, this is how he would die. Joseph was almost seven feet tall, and his skin was wrapped tightly around thick muscle. The hornbow in his left hand was as big as a Murickan longbow, and the bowie knife at his belt was longer than Levin's short sword. He wore the scars of many battles. Even with the confidence of youth on his side, Levin knew that he could not survive a fight with this man, but he had to try. He couldn't live with himself if he just allowed her to be taken away, to be used in, the Weaver only knew what ways.

"She belongs to me," Joseph said.

William came huffing up behind Levin, winded from running. He placed himself between the two men.

"Joseph," he said. "This is Levin, our clanbrother. He traveled with the woman before they were taken."

"She is mine by all our laws of property and honor," Joseph said. "I had claim to her before he was a member of the clan, you know this William."

William opened his mouth to speak, but Levin cut him off.

"I cannot let you take her," he said in a flat way that brooked no argument. It was fact. His guts churned, but he made himself stand up straighter. A laughable act, considering the monster of a man he was facing.

Joseph's thick brows curved down into a grimace, and his knuckles popped as his fist tightened around his hornbow. The sound was loud and menacing in the silence. Levin's heart pounded in his ears, and adrenaline made every nerve come to life with energy. Bile burned the back of his throat.

"Give me the spear," Joseph said.

Levin looked at Joseph, then at his halberd, then back at Joseph, uncomprehendingly.

After a long moment, the huge man said, "Ok, I'll throw in the bow." He handed the great hornbow to Mae, and gave her a gentle push toward Levin, then held out his hand.

In a disbelieving daze, Levin handed over the halberd and hugged Mae tightly. He heard Joseph talking to William behind him.

"Look at this, real wood!"

Levin pulled away from her and began to lead her away by the hand. He took three steps and bent over to vomit in the grass.

"Are you all right?" Mae asked.

"Yeah," he said, wiping his mouth with the back of his sleeve. "I thought I was going to die. I couldn't fight him and live. I can be brave at times, I guess, but I'm not an idiot."

"Die? Fight him? Why would you fight him?" Mae asked.

"I couldn't let him, or anyone, do... anything to you," he said, purposefully being vague.

"You were going to fight him for me?" Mae asked, with a strange tone to her voice.

He nodded. He hadn't had a choice. He couldn't just let them take her.

"And I suppose you would have done the same for anyone," she said, using his old words against him. She had a smile on her face and a sparkle in her eye though.

"No," he said simply.

"Well, for future reference, Joseph there, is one of the sweetest guys you're ever likely to meet. He just wanted me to do his laundry. The man has *seven* wives, and his fifth wife is lazy, or so he says. He wasn't going to do... anything to me except put me to work."

"*Seven* wives?" Levin asked incredulously.

"And 19 children," Mae said, and laughed. She sobered quickly and said, "But you were going to die for me. What am I to make of that?" She looked at him, she seemed to be enjoying the shy embarrassment on his face.

"I love you," he blurted, and instantly regretted it. The risk of rejection hung there like an executioner's blade. The most remarkable, beautiful, amazing creature that the Weaver had ever spun into his life, held the power to rip his heart out and destroy him with a laugh. A smirk or a giggle would send him spinning into madness, he feared. For one long, bleeding, painful second, his soul shrivelled. He had just faced certain death against a mountain of a man, and here he stood quailing in fear at the possibility that this perfect human being may not feel the same way.

"I," she began, and was interrupted by William.

"Come with me Levin, and I'll show you to your tent," he said, clapping Levin on the shoulder.

"I love you," she said, and kissed him fiercely. She kissed him the way he had always wanted to be kissed, with passion, desire, warmth, and affection. The kiss was love, friendship, devotion, and need. In that eternal moment, she was everything. She was the Web. Nothing else existed, nothing else mattered. She loved him. Those three words built a foundation under him and gave his life meaning.

"Ahem," William cleared his throat. "It's right over here."

They ignored him.

Chapter Eighteen

They broke their embrace after a long while, took each other's hand, and let William begin to lead them. Levin walked along as if in a dream. Happiness insulated him against the aches, pains, and worries of the world. William said something, but Levin was too far lost in thought.

"What was that?" Levin asked.

"I said, that was a very brave thing you did," William repeated.

"Brave? I was scared to death. Joseph would have killed me," Levin said.

"Bravery is not action instead of fear, it is action in *spite* of fear," William said, as if by rote. "Doing a thing without being afraid, is more often than not, stupidity. Facing our fear, and doing what we know to be right, is what sets us apart from the beasts of the field."

They walked along in silence for a short while, and came to a tent, no different from any of the others. Levin made a mental note to make a mark on it, so he wouldn't accidentally walk into someone else's tent in the future.

"Here you go," William said. "My tent is in the middle of the camp," he said pointing in an easterly direction. "Please join me at dusk," he said to Levin. "We should talk. Right now I have matters to attend to. There is a communal bull cooking on a spit, on the north side of camp, and a stream to the west, in case you get hungry or thirsty."

They said their farewells, and he left. Levin ducked inside the tent, and was pleased to find Delia already there. She ran up, arms flung wide, and hugged each of them. They hugged her back, and checked her for injuries. She was in perfect health. She explained to them that an old woman had brought her here, and told her to wait.

Levin stood up straight and looked around the tent. There was a small fire pit in the middle of the single round room. The tent covering was made of many cow hides and the frame consisted of about a dozen segmented poles. They looked like wood, but he had never seen any wood like that. The tent floor was covered in cow hides as well. There were pads, mats, cushions, and pillows up against the walls, all the way around, except for in front of the opening.

Delia walked over, got down on one of the cushions, and sat there quietly. She had always been a quiet child, but there was something about her now that puzzled him. If you ignored her random cryptic messages, she behaved like any other child, except that she didn't show any interest in playing with other children. Levin could hear children outside right now, laughing and screaming those high pitched squeals of childish glee. Delia showed no interest though, she just sat there quietly... doing what? He didn't know, and it bothered him. He had grown fond of the little girl, and it bothered him.

The concern must have shown on his face, because Mae put a hand on his shoulder and said, "What's wrong?"

"I'm just worried about Delia," he whispered, moving to the other side of the tent. "Before when we were traveling, we walked and slept. There was no time for anything else. Now though, she should be out there playing, or investigating, or whatever children do. Don't you think?" he asked.

She looked over at the little girl and nodded thoughtfully. "Yeah," she said. "It's almost like she's waiting."

"That's it! You're a genius," he said, then walked over to the princess, and sat down beside her.

"Delia," he said. "What are you waiting for?"

She turned her head to look at him, and blinked as if he'd pulled her out of deep thought. "Bashimaw," she said.

"What is that," he asked. "What does that mean?"

She just looked at him, but didn't respond. He shook his head in bewilderment, gave her a quick hug, and got to his feet.

"Does bashimaw mean anything to you?" he asked Mae.

She shook her head. Levin needed to relieve himself and pay William a visit. He said as much to Mae and ducked out of the tent. He felt her hand grab his elbow, and he turned around to find her standing behind him. She stepped close and kissed him. At first he wondered about his beard, and how she could stand it, then he got lost in her embrace.

"Be careful," she said, and ducked back inside. *I'm going to take a piss*, he thought, and shook his head in amusement. He looked around and decided to pull up a handful of grass. He rubbed it on the leather of the tent, just left of the door. It would mark his tent, so he could detect it among the others. For the first time since he arrived, he really had time to study the cowfolk. He walked slowly and looked at the people he passed. He could hear children playing from every direction. He saw many women, and a few men, carrying food, water, or laundry. Most of them had brown hair, but a few had either blond or black, and they wore it loosely flowing down their backs. As a rule, cowfolk had lighter skin than his own people. The older boys and girls wore their hair shaved on the sides, leaving a strip of hair down the center of their heads, from forehead to neck. The grown folk who weren't working, wore their hair in two unadorned braids. Most clothing was made from buckskin, a few older people wore some cloth, but no one wore armor that he could see.

Most people ignored him, but some shied away, looking frightened, and others stared openly. Children were as likely to run up to him and touch him, as they were to run away. The adults who wore braided hair almost always carried a cowfolk shield, a hornbow, and a quiver full of arrows. They all carried a long knife at their belts as well.

From his experience following them, he thought he knew their privy habits, so he headed south to their backtrail. Outside the camp, in the trail, he found several people squatting over holes or standing to relieve themselves. He felt a flush of relief as he emptied his bladder. The sun was starting to get low in the sky, so he headed to the center of camp, in search of William's tent.

He found it without much trouble. It was larger than the others, and he had been there before. There was nothing to knock on, so he just called out William's name, and entered when asked to do so.

"Come, come," William said, waiving him over, and leaning over to pat a cushion across from him. "Have a seat."

Levin saw that they were alone, and crossed the tent to sit down on the offered cushion. The man across from him was in his late forties or early fifties. He had kind dark eyes with deep crows feet in the corners. His smile was warm and inviting. Levin noticed tattoos on both of his hands, and the tip of his pinkie finger was missing on the left hand.

"I'm sure you have a lot of questions," William said, "and there are some things that I need to tell you. You ask your questions first, and I'll answer as best I can."

"You say I'm a proper member of the clan right?" William nodded. "Do I have duties, a job, work I'm supposed to do everyday?"

"We have hunters, warriors, defenders, and camp tenders. A person can be a hunter and a warrior, or a defender and camp tender, but you can't defend the camp while you're out hunting, or make war while you're tending the camp. Every person is responsible for their own tent and personal items. We keep a cow roasting on the big community fire, so no one goes hungry, but feel free to cook for yourself if you wish. Camp tenders and defenders, take care of the big fire and the community cooking. Hunters are self explanatory and it's normally young people who are warriors and want to go out on raids, to make a name for themselves. For now, you can concentrate on being a defender, until you figure out what you want to do.

I'll send Eric Swiftfellow to you. He can get you integrated into the guard rotation."

"What about Mae and Delia?" Levin asked.

"They belong to you. You can have them do your laundry and tan leather, or sell them if you wish. It's up to you. You are the only one who needs to contribute to the community, your property is your own."

"How did I become a member of the clan?" Levin asked.

"We have laws that are unbreakable. In the distant past, people would arm their slaves, and send them to defend the clan, an act of true cowardice. One slave defended the camp bravely several times, and was seen to do it. She was a brave woman, and had earned her freedom. So, the council came together at Baschima, and passed a law that made anyone who defended the clan with a weapon, became a member of the clan, and now owned the weapon they used. This stopped people giving their weapons to slaves and forcing them to fight."

"The axe that you used," William went on, "belonged to Henry Stonefist, the first gobner of the Stonesnakes. He was a great warrior, and it is said that strong spirits live in the axe."

"Mae told me that Joseph has seven wives. Is that true?" Levin said.

"Yes. I heard that your people marry one woman at a time, that seems strange to us. We may have as many wives as we wish. I had four, but Julie died last winter," William said a little sadly. "I have three now. Steve Longhorn has 11 wives. That is the most that I know of."

Just then, an old woman ducked into the tent, and looked startled at seeing them. "I'm sorry," she said. "I didn't know that you were still talking." She started to turn and leave, but William stopped her.

"No, no, come in please. I have someone I want you to meet." The old lady walked over and put her hand on William's shoulder. "Lidia," he said. "This is Levin, the newest member of the clan. He's the one that saved Sally and Billy." The old lady smiled broadly and nodded in greeting. "Levin, this is Lidia, my first wife."

"It's a pleasure to meet you," Levin said.

"Would you like something to drink," Lidia asked.

"No thank you," Levin replied.

"You have to try her tea. She makes the best tea south of the ice," William said.

"Ok," Levin said. "Thank you." The old woman went back outside.

"How long have you been together," Levin asked.

"I married her when I was about your age. It's been about 30 years now," William answered.

"I was born during the Bull Wars," Levin said. "I have heard many stories about it. What is Eye for an Eye, and is that why the cowfolk attacked?"

William looked thoughtful for a moment. "Yes, we hold to the truth that any person who is injured by another, should repay that injury with the same. If you kill one of the freefolk unjustly, that's what we call ourselves, every person injured by that murder is bound to repay it in kind. When your queen killed those three missionaries, she left us no choice but to cross the big river, something we are loath to do in large numbers."

"But I killed a woman in your tent. Why aren't her friends and family coming after me?" Levin asked.

"I said 'unjustly.' If the three missionaries had attacked someone and been killed in self defense, nothing would have come of it. They were hanged without provocation. Not only were their friends and family hurt by it, but many freefolk felt injured by the public way they were killed. This led to many more avengers than would be under normal circumstances," William explained.

"Oh ok," Levin said. "We have a saying in Muricka that goes, 'kill the lonely cowfolk.' It means to do a thing in the safest way possible," Levin said, and they both chuckled.

"In another moon cycle, we will be going to Baschima. It's the large permanent camp in the center of our lands. There you can become a member of the tribe," William said.

"I thought that I was already a member of the tribe," Levin said, confused.

"No, you're a member of this clan. Every person must go through the rights of passage to become an adult member of the tribe. By the tribal laws, you are like a child. You can own property, and perform duties, but you can't do anything official, like get married, vote on tribal affairs or hold a seat on any council."

"I understand," Levin said.

"When it comes time to move, everyone will be busy. We follow the Snake Herd, when they move, so do we. You'll need a horse to pull your tent, come find me when the time comes, and I'll help you as much as I can," William said. "The winters can be bad here, and if we get separated from our herd, we'll starve."

"All right," Levin said. "Thank you."

Lidia came back with the tea, and it was delicious. The age gap between her and William was larger than the one between Mae and himself. The thought made him feel good.

"It's great," he told her. "Thank you."

"Didn't I tell you," William said. "She makes the best tea."

They drank their tea, and ended the conversation with pleasantries. Levin thanked them profusely and walked back to his own tent. He had a lot to think about.

Chapter Nineteen

As he walked, he considered the prospect of becoming one of the cowfolk. He had always planned on returning to Muricka, and his family, as soon as he was sure that Delia was safe. Now, the Web had given him unexpected options. He would definitely want to talk to Mae about it. He wasn't sure about the medical proficiency of the cowfolk, but a good healer like Mae would be valued anywhere. He didn't think that he wanted to stay here, or become one of the cowfolk, but he liked to work over every option in his head, before making a decision.

Somehow he made it back to his tent in the dark. Mae and Delia were already asleep. He went out and gathered dried cow dung, from the large community pile near the center of camp, and quietly started a fire. He fell asleep quickly and woke up the next day feeling refreshed.

The next few days went by in a blur. He spent a lot of time with Mae, as much as possible, and spent the rest either walking a guard patrol or talking with William. Levin learned a lot about the cultural differences between the two peoples during those conversations. One morning upon meeting, William stuck his hand out with an expectant smile. Levin just looked at him uncomprehendingly. Then it struck him, William expected him to grab it with his own hand. It was bad luck to touch another person's hand in Muricka, especially someone who wasn't immediate family. Levin didn't want to offend this respected older man, who was becoming his friend, so he reached out and tentatively grabbed the offered hand. The older man pumped it up and down three times, and let it go, smiling.

There were many strange customs that Levin found unnerving. The men took as many wives as they wanted. He still hadn't wrapped his mind around that one. Why would anyone want more than one spouse? He was amazed and slightly disgusted when he found out that the cowfolk, or plainsmen rather, had sex outside of marriage. He asked William about it.

"Aren't you afraid of disease?" he had asked the older man.

"That is a possibility," William admitted, "but it's perfectly safe for two young people who are both virgins."

"How is it safe when the gods will curse them?" Levin asked.

"Gods curse them," William looked genuinely confused. "Diseases are spread by people, not gods. If the person you are with doesn't have a disease, you can't get one. Spirits live inside everything, and sickness spirits can move from person to person. Stone spirits keep an enemy's arrows from piercing the skin, wind spirits help a person to run swiftly, and sick spirits make us ill."

"Spirits?" Levin asked dubiously. He had never imagined that people could believe in anything other than the Web and the Weaver. Was this man crazy? Were these people crazy? The thought puzzled and even frightened him a little.

William nodded, and went on, "The spirits of the world guide us, strengthen us, make us sick, and sometimes kill us. The earth feeds us and the sky quenches our thirst."

Levin left that conversation deep in thought. He had a difficult time understanding how two people could hold such opposing views. He had known, his entire life, that sickness and disease were punishments placed on man by the Weaver, and sometimes the Father. The Mother never punished the human race. She was full of mercy and love. He went directly to Mae, and told her what he had learned. Her reaction was exactly what he expected.

"Everyone knows that the gods send disease as punishment," Mae said.

"Not long before I left, there was a man who stole some valuable things from the bethel. He fell sick the very next day, and returned what he'd stolen. A couple of days later, he was completely healed. Diseases are brought on by immoral behavior. How else would the gods make sure that we lived as decent people should?"

Mae was a webinar, one of the best healers in the realm, so he didn't argue with her. As he walked his rounds during guard duty, he puzzled over how two people can have opposite views, and both sound completely logical. He thought about it while practicing with sword and shield. He'd met Eric Swiftfellow, the captain of the guard, who introduced Levin to the other defenders and showed him where they practiced. Swiftfellow turned out to be a stooped old man, though, Levin supposed, he could have been swift in his youth.

In this way, the days turned into weeks and the moon went through its cycle. The time he spent with Mae, which was every free second he could find, was bittersweet. He cherished every moment spent with her, every conversation, or passing smile, but he wanted more. He wanted to be her husband and to sleep with her at night. He lay awake every evening, thinking of her body, the gentle curve of her hips, the swell of her breasts, her lovely bare feet, and the memory of their last kiss. They kissed often, but neither one of them was willing to go further before they were wed. It was torture wrapped in bliss.

Levin got to know the other defenders, and settled into a routine. Mae and Delia seemed to be content as well. Levin had seen Delia outside a few times, not playing with the other children, but just walking through the camp, observing. Most of the time she could be found in their tent, sitting cross legged, in a meditation-like state.

So the days passed, until the great herd began to move, and everything changed forever.

Chapter Twenty

The days were growing shorter, and it was chilly on the morning that they packed up. With the help of some people, and by observing others, the Murickan trio were able to get their tent taken down, rolled up, and tied to a horse. The tents were rolled up in such a way that they were able to place their belongings between the poles, and allow the horse to carry everything, except what they wore. It was a very fast and efficient way to travel. Within two hours, they were packed up and on the move, following the immense herd of wild cattle that were headed south for the winter.

Levin hadn't been invited to go out with any hunting party yet. That was one thing that he really wanted to do. He was curious about how they harvested meat from the massive herd, and wanted to experience it for himself. He was grateful for the chance to practice with his sword though. The plainsmen fought with a shield and a long knife, that they called bowies, he supposed because they carried it with a bow. His shortsword wasn't much longer than one of their knives, so sparring and training with the other defenders was an excellent way to gain experience. He was comfortable with his father's sword now, and could hold his own against any of his fellow defenders. The camp hadn't been raided since his first night there. He was grateful for that as well.

As they traveled, Levin noticed that women from all over camp came to Delia and exchanged whispers with her. He wondered about the odd behavior and asked the princess about it.

"Why do all of those women come to you?" he asked.

"They ask me questions," Delia said. She could be irritatingly brief at times.

"About what?" he asked.

"Their future," she said.

"What do you tell them?" he prodded.

"The truth," she answered. "Most of the time, I don't know anything about them."

"And the other times?" he asked.

The girl shrugged, and walked over to Mae, who was talking to a Stonesnake healer, and grabbed her hand, in a tacit signal that the conversation was over. Levin gave up and decided to find William. The older man was always good for a conversation. His luck was in, as he found the clan gobner walking alone.

"How far south do we travel," Levin asked him.

"Baschima is a couple of weeks travel. We will rest there for several days. All of the clans meet there each Spring and Fall. After that, we will catch back up with our herd and travel a couple of more weeks to the Winter grazing lands. We also gather our tent poles down south. There will be plenty to do once we get there."

"You have mentioned Baschima before. What is it?" Levin asked.

"Baschima is the closest thing that we Plainsmen have to a *town*," he pronounced the unfamiliar word slowly. "It's a permanent camp, the only one we have. Old people stay there year round, along with anyone else who can't travel. It's a holy place where the spirits gather, and people need to be there to tend them. It's also the place where the clans meet twice a year. Baschima is a place of peace. All violence is forbidden. The clans, mostly young people trying to earn a name for themselves, raid each other throughout the year, but never at Baschima. Anyone caught doing violence of any kind, no matter how high their rank, will be staked out on an ant hill, and left to die slowly. That has only happened once in my lifetime. We are nomads, and our society is loosely constructed, but our laws are iron."

"How many clans are there?" Levin asked.

"One hundred and forty eight named clans, and twice as many small bands," William said.

"A hundred and forty eight," Levin said, shocked. "Are they all as big as the Stonesnakes?"

"Oh, we are one of the smaller clans. The largest clan, the Big Hill clan, has more than twice our number, quite a bit more," William said.

"I had no idea that there were so many Plainsmen. Now the Bull Wars make more sense. I always believed that most of you came across the river, but now I know that it was a tiny fraction of Plainsmen who avenged the missionaries," Levin said.

"We Stonesnakes are a relatively peaceful clan, there are some who make war constantly. They take slaves and sell them across the mountains to the west," William said.

"There are more people to the west?" Levin asked. "More people besides the cowf... er, Plainsmen?"

"Yes," Willam answered. "We just call them Slavers. They speak differently from us, even more differently than you do. You can't understand anything they say, but they will buy slaves. They pay with strong drink, strong wood, and good furs. You will be able to tell the clans who trade with them, they dress differently than the rest of us. Beware them when you spot them, they are not to be trusted."

And so it went. Levin spent days talking with William and Mae. He learned about the customs of the Plainsmen, their culture and religion. Mae would spend her days talking to the healers and wise women of the clan, and they would compare notes. Mae was as stunned as he had been, at the sheer numbers of the Plainsmen, and at the news of the slavers to the west. He attempted to carry Delia on his shoulders for a while, but she got no enjoyment out of the action, so he didn't repeat it.

At last they came upon the Baschima. Levin should have been ready for it, but he was still shocked at the size of it. Tents filled the valley for as far as the eye could see. He stood there in the early afternoon sun, trying to imagine how many cattle died to make those leather tents, and could not. The numbers were just too large for his mind to grasp. The Stonesnakes had their own area where they pitched their tents every year. They went there now. They had slept under the stars most nights on their journey, but since they would be there for a few days, they set up their tents.

It felt wonderful to Levin to enter his tent again, and lie down under shelter. There was something to be said for sleeping under the stars, but it wore on a person after a while. One good thing about it though, it made you appreciate a roof, even a thin one. He reclined on his sleeping mat, hands beneath his head, closed his eyes and stretched his weary legs. He had never imagined that he might walk so far in his entire life as he had in the last few months.

He heard voices outside. Someone said his name. He got up wearily, and exited the tent. Mae and William were there talking. They looked at him and William said, "Come, come. The dancing is about to start."

Levin looked around for Delia. She was exiting the tent to join them. The group followed William as he wove his way between their temporary shelters, and into Baschima. Levin noted the construction of the permanent structures. They were similar to the smaller tents, except that the poles were larger, and they were buried in the ground. The largest of them was as big around as Mr. Wooler's sheep pasture, and this was the one they were headed to. People were entering from every direction, and milling around outside. They slowed to a stop as they got close, a sort of loose line was forming at the entrance.

"I don't know if it will be the Painted Dogs or the Watergrass clan that dances this year. They are both great, but I like the Painted Dogs," William said to Mae.

Three women walked out of the throng to join them. One of them Levin recognized from the evening in William's tent. Lidia, William's first wife. He recognized one of the other two, but couldn't remember her name.

"Mary, Lidia, and Kate, this is Levin, Mae, and... uh, where's Delia?" William said.

Everyone started looking around. She was nowhere to be seen. No one was really worried. She was surely ok, especially here in Baschima. It was more of an inconvenience. Still it was unlike the princess to go wandering off.

"I'll go find her and meet you inside," Levin said, and walked away, scanning the area. He moved in widening circles, calling her name and searching the crowd. Just as he began to worry, he found her exiting a medium sized tent that was luxuriant looking. It was covered in dark fur, instead of the usual tan leather.

"What were you doing in there?" he asked her. "I have been looking all over for you."

She looked up at him with those mysterious blue eyes, took his hand, and said nothing. Exasperated, he led her back to the entrance of the large tent. Their group was just entering. He watched them disappear inside, and hurried to catch up.

He couldn't see anything when he first entered the tent, it was dark inside. When his eyes adjusted, he was able to observe the layout of the structure. The center was comprised of a large round arena that was lit by many torches, with a raised platform at the center of it. There was enough seating for a thousand people around it, and it was filling up fast. Levin had no idea how he was going to find Mae and William among so many people, in the dark. He kept a hold of Delia's small hand and began to peer into the darkness, in a vain effort to locate his companions. He felt the little girl pulling on his jerkin, and looked down at her. She was pointing to his left. He looked that way and saw William coming toward them, waving his arms. They made their way to the older man, and followed him to the place where the others sat. Levin sat down with relief.

After several minutes, a procession of people carrying torches entered the tent. They walked to the dais and placed the torches in sconces around it. Levin could see that the people were painted from head to toe, one solid color, and otherwise naked. It took him a moment to sort it out, but there were four pairs of people, a man and a woman for each color, red, blue, yellow, and green.

"Painted Dogs," William whispered after nudging him in the ribs with an elbow.

Drums began to beat a rhythm from the darkness. There was a deep bass thump that you could feel in your seat, along with several lighter tapping and paddling sounds in accompaniment. The music was moving, Levin had never heard its like before. It made him want to move his feet.

The Painted Dogs spread out evenly around the circle, and began to dance. Their movements were smooth and fluid. The cobbler back home was the richest man in town. He owned a painting that Levin supposed was beautiful. It depicted a knight in battle with a fierce dragon. He was not completely ignorant to the fact that people could create beautiful works of art, but it had never occurred to him that movement could be beautiful, until now.

The dancers flowed from one position to the next. They turned the flexing of muscles and the bending of joints into an artform. They began to take turns on the dais. One of the dancers would walk up the platform and begin to spin and girate in such an erotic way that Levin's cheeks began to burn, and he specifically did not look at Mae. He tried not to imagine her painted blue and moving like that, but he failed.

As he watched and tried to look unperturbed, and once again failing, he noticed some movement in front of him. It looked as though someone were moving toward the dancers, but it was hard to tell in the dark. Eventually, someone stepped out of the audience and into the torchlight of the arena.

It was Delia.

Chapter Twenty One

The smaller drums stopped playing when Delia entered the circle, but the bass kept playing, in perfect rhythm with her small steps. Boom, Boom, Boom, it went, every time her foot touched the ground. The dancer who was occupying the dais, stepped back as Delia approached. Boom, Boom, pounded at the rafters of the pavilion with each step of the platform. Finally, as she stepped onto the top of the platform, the drumming stopped. The silence was deafening.

The princess walked to the center of the raised wooden stage, and began to turn in a circle. Her eyes swept the crowd slowly. As her gaze passed over Levin, it seemed as if their eyes locked, and for a sliver of eternity, she looked inside him. He felt as if he'd been weighed and measured, mind and soul. There was no wind, no crickets chirped, no horses whinnied, there was only silence, as every person, and seemingly every *thing*, held their breath. It was as if the entire Web was waiting to hear what she had to say. She stopped turning in the exact spot that she had begun. She slowly raised her tiny hands, and began to speak.

"I am the Heart of the Herd," she said. Her voice had changed, in a way, but not really. If you changed a wooden spoon into a steel spoon, it would still be a spoon, just harder and colder, and... different. That was how her voice had changed. "I am the Cold Wind, and the Prairie's Soul," she intoned. Her words were crystal clear, as if they weren't affected by the miniscule variances in vibrating air molecules, as if she were speaking directly into Levin's head. "I will save the Plainsmen, and I will destroy you."

A guttural panicked scream tore through the air. A man sprang from the crowd and ran toward Delia. Levin stood up, although there was nothing he could do, he was too far away. The man carried his bowie in his fist, and was at the edge of the circle in three long strides, his knife pumping up and down with the motion of running, and his long legs kicking back. The little princess didn't even look in his direction as he tripped on the circle border and went sprawling. His knife plunged through his throat when he hit the ground, the blade protruded from the back of his neck, and gleamed wetly as he twitched the remainder of his life away.

A thousand voices raised at once, but Levin couldn't tell if it was happiness, hatred, or fear that he heard. The crowd got to its feet and surged forward. Levin was pushed from behind as people pressed past him. He started to move forward with them, in an attempt to get to the little girl on the dais, but William's hand on his arm stopped him. The noise was too loud for them to talk, but Levin understood at once that the effort was futile. There was absolutely nothing he could do against a thousand people.

Levin grabbed Mae by the hand and followed William outside. The pavilion walls were thin, so even out here, they had to yell to hear each other.

"What the Web is going on?" Levin asked.

"I don't know, but I know where we can find out," William said, and motioned for them to follow. The noise grew slightly dimmer and more distant as they sped past smaller tents. Levin stopped as William walked up to the only tent that he recognized. It had dark supple fur covering, in place of the standard leather.

"What's wrong," Mae asked.

"Remember when Delia disappeared earlier?" Levin asked. Mae nodded. "Well, this is where I found her. She was coming out of this tent."

"Are you sure?" she asked.

"Positive. Look at the fur. There's not another tent like it."

William turned around at the entrance and motioned for them to hurry. They walked inside and found a lone podium, with a single book sitting on it. There was no smoke hole in this tent, as in most others. William went to the book, and began flipping through it. The book was large, four feet across when it was open, and almost as tall. The cover was dark leather. The pages were thick and seemed to be made of animal skins. They were covered in a small neat script of black ink, though there were a few illustrations that Levin saw.

"Ah, here it is," William said. He began to read aloud, "The Heart of the Herd will be born of fire and fear. She will follow the setting sun, bringing eleven and one." He looked at Mae and said, "She only came with the two of you, right?"

"He is Eleven," Mae said, pointing at Levin, a disbelieving look on her face. Levin explained how he got his name when it was clear that the gobner didn't understand.

"Spirit of fire," William whispered in astonishment. He went back to the book and began to read again. "She will break the horn and the bow. The clans will sunder if they do not bend. She will save us from our doom, and destroy us. She walks through tomorrow as the spider walks over the web, while others are trapped in today."

"What does all that mean?" Mae asked.

"It's called the Cold Wind Prophecy. It is supposed to herald the end of the clans," William said. "There are as many interpretations as there are Plainsmen. It is suggested that she will both destroy and save the clans. Obviously, the man with the knife believed that she would destroy us. That's the thing about prophecy, if you could change it, it wouldn't be prophecy. Trying to change an actual prophecy is like trying to milk a calf."

"Well, what do we do?" Mae asked Levin.

"Right now, we need to see if we can find her, and see if she's ok. I don't know if that mob worshiped her, or ripped her apart," Levin said.

"Don't say that," she said, and gave him a light smack on the shoulder. "She has to be ok. Let's go find her."

The three of them left the tent, and walked back toward the pavilion together. They all stopped suddenly at the sight of Delia walking along, with one thousand people behind her. The princess looked directly at them as she passed, but said nothing. Levin knew that she would simply ignore anything he said to her, but Mae tried.

"Delia," she called. Nothing. They looked at each other and shrugged. "Well," Mae said. "I think that we should wait for everything to settle down, then try to talk to her. We need to know what she's doing. We came all this way for her, now what do we do?"

"I need to find my wives. I didn't see any of them in the group that was following her. I'm heading back to Stonesnake grounds," William said, and started walking. The other two fell in behind him.

"This is unbelievable," Mae said. "I don't know what to think, let alone what to say or do."

"Getting her here safely was our goal, and we accomplished it. She is safe, and her uncle can't touch her," Levin said.

They talked as they made their way to their tent. Once there, Levin gathered fuel and started a fire. There was a chill in the air tonight. The light and warmth given off by the fire was welcome. They sat close to the fire and close to each other.

"We have to go back," said Mae.

"Go back?" asked Levin. "Do you think so?"

"Think about it," Mae said. "She is the rightful queen, and now she has a huge army at her back. They have been content to stay over here and fight each other, up until now, but if they believe that she is this, Heart of the Herd, they will follow her. It will be the Bull Wars all over again, except a thousand times worse."

"You're right," Levin said. "There's no way that she will go back with us. It would be suicide as long as her uncle is alive, plus she's basically a queen to the cowfolk. If we know they're coming, maybe we can stop them at the river, and prevent a slaughter. Still, maybe we should ask her what she plans on doing. She might intend to take the clans west."

"She might have us taken prisoner, and then what?" Mae asked.

"They cannot do violence here. Not even to take our weapons and tie us up. It is forbidden. This may be our only chance to safely find out what she intends to do," Levin said.

"Yes, you're right, let's do that first thing in the morning. We need to find out what's going on before we make any decisions."

"I want to go back regardless," Levin said, as his heart began to beat faster. "I know that it would mean for you to give up the faith, and being a webinar, but I couldn't live with myself if I didn't ask. I could die tomorrow, and I don't want that to happen without you knowing how much I love you. I want you to come home with me and become my wife. Will you marry me Mae?"

She didn't answer right away, she just looked at the fire, so he went on in a rush, "You could still be a healer. You could still do what you love, it just wouldn't be at a bethel. I would," she cut him off.

"Yes," she said, looking at him. The firelight danced on the tears forming in her beautiful eyes. "Yes."

Levin embraced her. It was awkward because they were both sitting on the floor, but it was warm and amazing. It was love. He kissed her thoroughly, happiness swelling inside him.

"We can leave tomorrow, after we talk to Delia," Levin said.

"You can probably trade that big bow that Joseph gave you for a couple of horses," Mae said. "It will make the journey a lot faster and easier."

"Great idea," Levin said. "I'll never use that thing anyway. It's too big."

Levin stoked the fire and they laid down to sleep. It was a long time coming though, in light of what had happened. Levin babbled about the future. He told her of the house he would build for them, and about the spot of land he had picked out last summer. He hadn't known her then, but he had known that he would build a house one day, and he had fallen in love with one spot of land the second he saw it. It was about a 15 minute walk from the village. It had a clear stream with a beaver's dam making a pond. He had pictured a house next to the pond, with a garden and a couple of donkeys. Now, he supposed, that they might have horses. It was possible. He closed his eyes and pictured it again, this time with horses, and Mae standing in the garden. It was paradise.

Finally they fell asleep with smiles on their faces and love in their hearts. The thoughts of possible war, butchery, and prophecy were somehow overshadowed by the prospect of love and marriage.

Chapter Twenty Two

They woke up the next morning and set out to find William. He would know where to find Delia, and who might be interested in the large hornbow. They found him outside his tent, talking to one of his wives. He greeted them as they approached.

"Hey William," Levin said. "Do you know where Delia is? We need to talk to her."

"From what I've been told, she's taken up residence in the Spirit Hut on the west side of the valley. It's made of mud and grass, you can't miss it," William said.

"I'd like to trade this for a couple of horses," Levin said, holding up the bow.

"You could get half a dozen horses for that bow. Horns like that are hard to come by, horses aren't," William said.

"We only need two," Levin said. "Well, maybe three. We could use one as a pack horse."

"I'll give you three young mares for it right now. You'll get your horses and I'll be able to make a profit," William said.

Mae's haggling spirit rose within her, and she started to speak, but then thought better of it. The man was doing them a favor, and it wouldn't be polite to squeeze more out of him. Three horses was worth a small fortune back home in any case.

"It's a deal," Levin said, and handed the bow to the older man. "We can collect the horses after we talk to Delia, if that is alright with you."

"No problem," William said, holding up the bow, inspecting it appreciatively. "There will be a council meeting of clan gobners, but that's not until this afternoon. We need to figure out what we're going to do, after Delia's revelation."

"We should be back before noon," Mae said, and the pair walked away to the west, looking for the grass hut.

"Spinning webber," Levin said. "Three mares! Your idea is even better than I thought. We can breed them when we get back home. We're rich!"

"There's a reason horses are rare back home," Mae said, tempering his excitement a little. "The winters are long and we don't migrate south. It's hard to keep large animals alive for so long. Horses are more susceptible to disease than donkeys, raising horses is hard."

"We'll figure it out," Levin said optimistically. "However you look at it, three horses is better than no horses."

Mae shook her head and smiled. His optimism was one of the things that she loved about him, but it could be exasperating at times.

"Is that it?" Levin said, pointing.

Mae looked in the direction he was pointing and saw a large grass structure. The grass was green and swaying in the breeze, making the hut seem almost alive. William had said that the building was made of mud and grass, but Mae hadn't expected the grass to be growing. She had envisioned something dead and quite a bit less animated. The hut was large, probably one third the size of the pavilion, and the entrance was straddled by two armed guards. This was also surprising. It wasn't the way of the cowfolk to set personal guards, especially here in Baschima, where violence was strictly prohibited. Mae wondered what the guards would do if Delia was threatened somehow. In the center of each shield was a large green heart.

"Is Delia here?" Mae asked the guards when they were within conversational distance.

The guard on the right jerked her head toward the entrance, in a signal for them to enter. They ducked their heads and went inside. The interior was sparsely decorated, but well lit with torches. The smoke left black streaks of soot on the mud ceiling. Pads and cushions lay neatly along the wall, and in the center of the room was a large rectangular chest, made of the same wood as the tent poles.

Delia sat cross legged in the back of the room, on a large cushion. Her eyes were close and she had a calm expression on her face. Mae and Levin walked over and sat down facing her.

"Delia," Levin said. The little girl opened her eyes and looked at him. "What's going on? We risked our lives to get you here, we deserve to know what we did it for."

The little girl looked at him, unblinking, for so long that Mae began to think that she wasn't going to answer. She had never spoken very much, and was known to ignore direct questions put to her. Finally, she did answer, though her answer wasn't much more enlightening than her silence had been.

"I am where I am supposed to be. This is my destiny and yours. I have nothing to give you as a reward for fulfilling your destiny, but if you want my thanks, you have it." The princess had never acted much like a child, but now the little girl was completely gone. It was eerie to hear those words, with that inflection, coming from the mouth of a child.

"We are trying to decide what to do now," Mae said. "We need to be sure that you are safe, but we also have lives to live."

"You will follow your destiny, as you always have, as do we all. I am safer here than I ever have been," the princess said.

"Are you going to stay here?" Levin asked.

Delia looked at him for a long moment, "Muricka is mine." She said it as if she were talking about a pair of shoes, or a hair brush.

Insanely, the thought of strangling her right there and then, flashed through Levin's mind. How many would die if she crossed the Big Sip with an army? How many would he save by ending it right now? He had come to terms with the fact that he was a killer. He was a good soldier, and could do his duty, but cold blooded murder was beyond him, especially when the victim was a little girl. He shook his head to dispel the image.

Mae got to her feet and Levin followed suit. The little girl was obviously safe here, that was the most important immediate concern. Mae didn't want to reveal too much about their plans, in the event that Delia would send cowfolk to intervene. She spontaneously bent down and hugged the girl, in one last gesture of warmth to the little princess she had rescued forever ago, in the bowels of the castle. She stood and they left without another word. In her vague and cryptic way, the princess had made everything clear. They knew what they must do.

They found William at his tent, and after waiting for him to finish giving instructions to a young boy, he led them to his horses, which were staked out on the side of a sloping hill. To Levin's great surprise and delight, a young appaloosa filly was among them. Levin went to her immediately and asked if she could be one of them.

"Any three you want," William said.

Mae chose a chubby bay, and they agreed on a sleepy sorrel filly for their pack horse. They led the animals back to camp and staked them outside their tent. Levin set out to see about acquiring a couple of saddles and Mae started packing their things. Levin went back to William one more time to ask about saddles.

"You forget," the older man said. "Our clan's sacred axe still belongs to you. Go to the supply tent, and take what you need from the community stores, and I will tell the council that you returned ownership of the axe to us."

Levin had forgotten about the axe. He had returned it to its rightful place in William's tent, and hadn't thought about it since. He went to the supply tent and took two riding saddles and a pack saddle. There were dozens of them to choose from. He also grabbed a few other things that they would need on their journey, a couple of bridles, lead ropes, a skinning knife, a sharpening stone, a hoof pick, and a horse brush. He knew that the axe was worth far more than the few items that he had taken, but Levin didn't want to feel as if he'd taken advantage of these people who had been so kind to him.

When he got back to the tent, he saddled the horses and helped Mae finish packing. They took four of the leather pieces that made up the outside of the tent. William told them that their tent would be dismantled if they left it, so it wouldn't hurt to start the process. The large pieces of leather would come in handy if it rained. After they got everything packed up, they said their goodbyes. They did not return to the grass hut. William and his wives bid them safe travel and asked the Spirits to guide them.

The sun was high in the sky when they set off to the east. Neither one of them had much experience riding a horse, but they would learn along the way. Levin had learned to fight by fighting, so he supposed that this couldn't be much more difficult, and a whole lot safer. If you made a mistake in the shield wall, your reward was a hole in the ground and a faceful of dirt. To his chagrin, Mae learned much faster than he did. By the second day, she seemed as if she'd been born in the saddle.

He decided to name his mare Shawnee. He couldn't remember where he'd heard the name, but he liked it. Mae named her bay mare Kimmie, and they couldn't agree on a name for the pack horse. Levin liked Proudwind, but Mae wanted something more feminine and cute, like Cherry. Levin didn't like the idea of naming an animal after fruit, but he knew that Mae would probably get her way. At the end of the day, it didn't matter, and he wanted her to be happy.

The trip back was a lot more enjoyable than the original journey. Riding a horse was a lot more fun, and less taxing, than walking had been, not to mention faster. He was constantly searching the land around them for signs of danger. They had seen lions the first time, but they had been on foot. The lions may be more likely to attack a horse. They made it to the river though, without incident. The river, however, did present a new kind of problem. How to get the horses across? Levin absolutely *dreaded* the idea of leaving them behind. After talking about it, they decided to travel up river and try to find a way across. The time saved by riding, afforded them a few days to search, and the value of the horses compelled them to do everything possible in order to keep them.

On the morning of the second day, they came to a place where the river widened and the water slowed down. It was more than twice as wide, but not nearly as deep or fast. After discussing it, they decided that it wouldn't hurt to try. They rode their mounts into the water and began to cross. It was no more than chest deep on the horses, most of the way. The little mares were forced to swim a few times, but the crossing was fairly easy.

"This must have been how the cowfolk crossed during the Bull Wars," Levin said.

"Yeah," Mae said, nodding assent. "You can see the water line, where the river gets to during spring, when the snow melts." She pointed to a spot on the bank. "But right now, it's wide and shallow enough to take an army across."

The crossing took up the better part of a day. The sun was low in the sky when they got to the other side. They decided to make camp and dry out. There was plenty of wood on this side of the river, and Levin was happy to be able to make a proper fire once more. That evening, they sat beside a crackling fire, and talked.

"You know that you can still be a healer after we are married. Healers are important people in towns and villages," Levin said.

"Yes, I know, but there is a lot more to being a webinar than just healing," Mae said.

"Oh really?" Levin asked earnestly. "Like what?"

"We pass down old knowledge, like the earth is the third planet from the sun, and you can make gumpowder out of bat manure," Mae said.

"What's gumpowder?" Levin asked.

"I don't know. No one does, but many webinars have experimented with bat manure to try to make it," Mae said.

"Really?" Levin asked, fascinated. "What else?"

"You can use magnets and copper to make energy," Mae said.

"What's a magnet?" Levin asked.

"It's a rock that sticks to iron," Mae said.

"What kind of energy, like fire?" Levin asked.

"No one knows," Mae said. "Webinars are always experimenting with things, trying to figure out what the old knowledge means. Some have been successful, like the windmill and the water wheel for grinding grain, or the compown bow. Lord Compown keeps that knowledge close to the chest though. Lots of things that we take for granted came from knowledge passed down through the Webinary, steel, paper, cotton, wool, and the knowledge of diseases, are just a few."

"I always wondered why everyone knew how diseases were spread," Levin said.

"We have webinars who's only job is to copy information so that we can continue to pass it down," Mae said. "Some webinars are healers, some are farmers or herders, and some are traders. It's just that the healers are the most common, and well known. People don't normally interact with the Webinary unless they need help or want to join."

"It is said that long ago there was an age of information, when people could use the Web to create anything and to talk to each other from anywhere, but they had casual sex and almost destroyed the planet with their greed and lust, so the Weaver sent diseases to wipe them away. The Weaver could have wiped us all away, but he spared some of us to start over again. Some of those people who lived were the first webinars. They gathered knowledge to pass down. The remaining humans were little more than animals, scavenging and hunting. We had lost the ability to farm and make things, but the Webinary kept the information safe, and now we are trying to help people live better lives, without the mistakes of our past," Mae said.

Levin enjoyed these conversations. Mae's intelligence fascinated him as much as her beauty. They talked into the night and fell asleep beneath the stars.

Chapter Twenty Three

Three days later they arrived at Levin's home town of Brookville, and they brought winter with them. Snow was falling as they rode up to uncle Remi's house and dismounted. The snow dampened all sound, and the village was unnaturally quiet this evening. They tied their horses to the log fence and knocked on the door. Aunt Tilda looked at him in bemusement for a short moment, then recognition and delight lit up her face. She squealed, and laughed, and threw her arms around his neck.

"Penny," she called. "Alek is back!"

His mother came running and flung herself at him. She hugged him so fiercely that breathing was difficult.

"I'm so glad you're ok," she said. Tears of joy ran down her cheeks as she stepped back to get a look at him. He was suddenly conscious of his scruffy beard and long hair. She took in their buckskin clothing and then her gaze went to the horses. "It looks like you have done well for yourselves."

She stepped back to make room for them to come inside. Levin noticed right away that the thatch had been replaced in the ceiling. His uncle sat at the table, and gave him a big smile.

"Welcome home son," Remi said, and winced as he shifted in his seat.

"Are your wounds still bothering you?" Levin asked.

"Oh, no," his uncle said. "A donkey stepped on my foot, I think my toe is broken." He stuck his foot out for them to see. The big toe on his right foot was swollen and an angry red.

"Ouch," Mae said. "That looks painful." She walked over and gave the man a hug.

"You're supposed to put a shoe on the donkey, not a donkey on your shoe," Levin said, and his uncle laughed good naturedly.

"Sit," aunt Tilda said. "I'll get us something to drink. We want to hear all about your adventures."

Mae and Levin sat in the two empty chairs, and began their tale. Every so often they were interrupted with a question like, what kind of axe, or how big were the lions. The three listeners were most stunned by the fact that the cowfolk didn't pray to the Weaver or even know about the Web.

"I heard that their missionaries had strange ideas, but I had no idea how strange," uncle Remi said.

They ended their tale with the river crossing. Then sat back to answer questions.

"What do the slavers look like," Tilda asked.

"We don't know, we never saw them," Mae said.

"Which wife does the man sleep with, when he has more than one?" his mother asked.

"I don't know, I never asked," Levin said laughing.

"You never got to see the great herd up close?" Remi said. He seemed as fascinated as Levin had been, with the sheer numbers of animals and people.

"No," Levin answered. "I wanted to go on a hunt, but I never got the chance. I was a camp defender. I did get a lot of practice with my sword though."

"Do you think that the princess can see the future?" Tilda asked.

"I believe so," Levin said, and at the same time Mae said, "I don't think so." They looked at each other and smiled. They hadn't really talked much on the subject.

"I'm just glad you made it home safely," Penny said. "I have been worried sick about you."

It was dark and late by the time their story was told, and all of the questions had been answered. Levin went outside to see to their horses. He tied a leather piece over each of their backs to keep them free from snow. Then he gathered a couple of armloads of firewood. It would be a cold night, and his uncle was injured. He and Mae pulled out their bedrolls and picked a warm spot on the floor to sleep. As he was unrolling his bedding next to Mae's, he saw his mother watching him with a concern on her face and a faraway look in her eyes. She smiled when she noticed him looking at her, and turned to go into the kitchen. They said their goodnights and went to sleep. For the first time in a long time, Levin slept peacefully.

Levin was the first one to wake the next morning. He stoked the fire to push back the morning chill. He used the quiet time to think. He knew that he wanted to marry Mae as soon as possible, but he also needed to warn someone about the cowfolk. Who to warn though, and would he even be believed? His story was a fair patch beyond believable. He reckoned that the answer to his question was simple when you boiled it down. He only knew one person to tell. The real question was, whether or not Lord Bracken was still alive. He would marry Mae, then go to the Falcon Keep, to talk to Lord Bracken.

That prospect brought up more questions though. He was, technically, still the lord's squire. He supposed, after some thought, that he was a soldier though. That is how he would make a living. He could do well as a soldier, give Mae a good life. He could not imagine going back to smithing or farming after what he had experienced. Battle was life on the edge of a knife. There were no questions at the end of a battle. If you were alive, and your opponent was dead, you did well. There wasn't any subjective element. Battle was black and white. The Weaver erases all shades of gray from the battlefield, leaving it spiritually clean.

He saw Mae begin to wake up, and knelt beside her to kiss her forehead.

"Good morning, beautiful," he whispered.

"Good morning," she mumbled and rubbed her nose, then went outside to use the outhouse. He went with her and checked their horses, then used the privy after her. He thought about feeding the horses all winter, and knew that Mae had been right about the horses. It would not be easy to keep them alive, let alone breed more. He supposed they could sell the pack horse to buy food enough for the other two, that would get them through the first winter.

"You dead in there?" it was Uncle Remi's voice. "It's spinning cold out here!"

Levin shook himself off and laced up his britches. Uncle Remi was standing there shaking when he opened the door. Remi limped into the outhouse and Levin walked through the fresh snow back to the house. He was greeted with the smell of fresh coffee when he opened the door. Aunt Tilda and Mae were sitting at the table, and his mother was making coffee. She brought a cup over to him. It was delicious. The cowfolk had tea, but no coffee. He hadn't realized how much he'd missed it.

"Were the cowfolk out of sharp steel?" his mother asked him, gesturing at his beard. He blushed and glanced at Mae.

"No," Levin said. "I just figured I'd give it a try."

"Well," Penny said, "at least it's full, not patchy like the butcher's son Jit."

"I think it looks good," Mae said, smiling at him.

He smiled back, and walked over to stand beside her, leaving the last chair for his injured uncle.

"I hate to ask Alek," Aunt Tilda began.

"Levin," his mother interrupted. "His name is Levin, remember?"

"I'm sorry. I hate to ask you Levin, but do you think you could give your uncle a hand today? He is falling behind because of his foot, and he could really use some help."

"Of course," Levin said. He had helped his uncle many times over the years. It was familiar, if boring, work. "I'd be happy to help."

"Thank you A... uh Levin," his aunt said, clapping her hands and bouncing in her chair a little. Remi came through the door and stamped his good foot, shivering and rubbing his upper arms. "Levin said that he will give you a hand today," Tilda said.

It took a second for him to put the name with his nephew.

"Thanks Levin," he said, the name new on his tongue.

For a moment Levin almost regretted changing his name, and the confusion it caused. He had earned that name though, and it had belonged to his father as well. It just felt right. Everyone else would have to get used to it. He didn't ask very much from others, and he hoped that they wouldn't begrudge him over this.

Penny brought out his old winter coat. It was a little small now, but its warmth would be welcome. After they finished their coffee, Levin and his uncle left for work, as did Tilda. Aunt Tilda cared for an old couple up the road. Their children were prosperous and paid her to tend them a few days a week. Mae helped with the dishes and rolled up their bedding. She really liked Penny, and was looking forward to talking with her.

Penny had a fresh cup of coffee waiting for her when she sat down.

"Thank you," Mae said.

"You're welcome. So, you and Levin have been through a lot together," Penny said.

"Yes," Mae said. "He's a wonderful man. I want to thank you for raising such a good person. You can't imagine how selfless and brave he is. I wish you could see him like we saw him out there in the wilderness. You would be so proud."

"I am proud," Penny said, but the tone of her voice didn't convey pride. "I'm going to be blunt with you. I need to get this off my chest. You're too old for him. You're going to die years before him, and he will be left alone. I know what it's like to be left alone. I know what it's like to lose the one you love most in this world, and I don't want that for my son!" she almost yelled the last part.

Mae was surprised by the words and the emotional outburst. She hadn't thought about any of that. She just knew that she loved Levin, and wanted to spend the rest of her life with him. Penny just looked at her, waiting for her to speak.

"I love him," Mae said, simply and truthfully.

"Of *course* you love him," Penny said with more than a little venom. "He's a wonderful *boy.*" She unmistakably stressed the last word. "You're ten years," Penny began.

"Eleven," Mae interrupted.

"Eleven years older than him," Penny corrected. "That's eleven years he'll live after you die. Do you want him to spend the last decade of his life alone?"

Mae didn't answer, she just looked at the coffee cup in her hands. Of course she didn't want him to be alone. She wanted Levin to be happy. She needed him to be happy, because her own happiness was entwined with his. The thought of him growing old, all by himself, upset her. Everything in the world was complicated and dangerous. Levin was the one thing in her entire life that was simple and sweet, until now.

What was she supposed to do? She silently prayed to the Father for guidance, and her stomach churned at the thought that Penny may very well be the Father's guidance. She stood up without a word, and went outside. She had some thinking to do.

Chapter Twenty Four

Levin thought of Mae as he walked back to the house with his uncle. This had been the longest stretch of time that he'd spent away from her in months. He had never been what you'd call a people person. He was very comfortable in solitude, and uncomfortable spending much time among other people, especially large groups. Mae had been different though. He'd never felt uncomfortable around her. Having the choice to spend time in her company or in solitude, he would choose her company, and she was the only person who he could say that about. Spending time with his uncle, or even his mother, had been like scratching his head. It felt good at first, but after a while, it would become irritating and even unbearable. It had always been his nature to spend long stretches of time by himself.

That is why his feelings for Mae surprised him. They went beyond lust or friendship, to what could only be love. He loved her as much as he loved himself, even more when he thought about it. He would put himself in harm's way to protect her. He would gladly take any pain upon himself, to spare her the hurts. The big, fat, sparkling jewel in his crown of happiness, was the fact that she loved him back. This beautiful, incredible, intelligent woman loved him! He had always known that he would fall in love and marry one day. He would find a wife to spend his life with, and treat her with gentle kindness. He'd just never dared to imagine that the woman could be someone like Mae, with her curly brown hair, beautiful smile, and sharp wit. Everyday since they had declared their love for each other, had been a bit surreal for him, like he could wake up at any moment.

They made it back to the house, and Levin revelled in the tingling warmth when they got through the door. He stamped his feet and took off his coat. He looked around for Mae, but didn't see her.

"Where's Mae?" he asked.

"Hmmm?" his mother mumbled, not looking around. "Oh, she left."

Levin's mind reeled and his heart beat loudly in his ears.

"What do you mean, left? Where did she go, and when did she leave?" he asked his mother.

"Not long after you left this morning. She walked outside and hasn't returned," she said, not looking up from the dishes.

"What did you say to her? She wouldn't just leave," Levin was near panic now. His heart raced and he felt nauseous.

"I just told her the truth, that she is too old for you. I don't want you to be old and alone, I just want to see you happy," she said, finally looking at him.

He was seized by a crazy image of drowning her in that dirty dishwater. The temerity, the utter *gall*, she displayed at sticking her nose into his relationship with Mae. He loved his mother, but in that instant he hated her with a fierce passion. He walked over and grabbed his knapsack, Mae had repacked it this morning. He saw her bag next to his, and grabbed it too. Mae must have been really upset to have left her bag behind. He imagined her walking off, into the cold, having done absolutely nothing wrong, except to love him.

"What are you doing?" Penny asked.

"I'm going to find Mae," Levin said. "She is my life. Without her I have nothing, I am nothing, and nothing matters." There were tears in his eyes as he walked to the door. He turned around as he opened the door and said to his mother, "You'd better hope I find her, if you ever want to be forgiven for this." She started to say something, but the slamming door cut her off.

As he was saddling Shawnee, he heard the door open, and looked up to see his uncle hobbling toward him. He was upset beyond words, but he didn't want to take it out on his uncle. They had spent a pretty good day together.

"I'm sorry son," his uncle said. "She didn't mean anything by it. She loves you and was trying to protect you. You are always going to be her little boy. Just remember that, huh?"

"I hate her so much right now," Levin said, wiping tears from his cheeks.

"I know, but it will pass, if you let it. She's a good woman, and her heart was in the right place, even if her head wasn't. She will be a good mother-in-law to Mae, if you give her a second chance."

Levin nodded and gave his uncle a hug, then mounted his horse.

"You go find that pretty girl now, and bring her back here so I can look at her some more," his uncle said with a smile.

"I will," Levin said as his uncle started to limp back to the house. "Uncle Remi," the older man turned to look at him. "I love you, and thanks," he put his heels into Shawnee's ribs and galloped away without waiting for a response.

There was only one way she could have gone, and that was east. He pushed his mount hard at first, but slowed down after a while. He had to figure out what to do. One good thing was that he knew about how far she could walk in the given time. She was out here alone though, without even a coat. She had walked off with nothing but what she wore. Anger at his mother surged up inside him again. How could she be so cold and thoughtless? How could she be so selfish and intrusive? He had entertained an idea of Mae and his mother being the best of friends, cooking and healing together. He would build an extra room on the house for his mother. They could take care of her in her old age. Now, he wanted her to be cold and alone, instead of Mae. He tried to think about his Uncle Remi's advice and calmed down again. Impudent anger wasn't going to help the situation.

After he had travelled further than he knew that Mae could have, he stopped and thought for a bit. Going any further would be a waste of time, he knew that. A quarter of a mile farther east, the road split in three directions, and his odds for picking the wrong one were pretty good. He couldn't believe the position he was in. Now he found himself becoming angry with Mae. How could she be so careless? How could she leave him without a word? She had to know that he would come after her. Maybe she didn't love him after all. If she had, she wouldn't have been able to leave him, right? He couldn't make himself believe that. He knew that she loved him, people did stupid things, even smart people like Mae.

The sun was setting, it would be dark soon. Levin decided the only thing to do was to camp at the fork in the road and wait. Maybe he would get lucky. He started east again. This was going to be one miserable night. Snow on the ground and worry in the heart. His horse hadn't eaten all day, and he felt guilty about that. When he got to the fork, he tied Shawnee under a big tree. The ground underneath it was fairly dry. The snow couldn't make it past the umbrella of needled limbs. That was a small thing to be thankful for.

He looked around in the fading light, for something to feed his horse. He scraped away snow and was able to find a few handfuls of grass, but the real prize was an apple tree that still had a few withered apples on it. He picked every one and took them, along with the grass, back to Shawnee. She ate gratefully. She had turned out to be a good horse, with a personality of her own. She was motivated by food, and aggressive. She would lay back her ears and go after Kimmie when the other horse got close to her food. During their return trip, he had started staking her further away from the other horses, to avoid any confrontations.

After she had eaten the last apple, he pulled out his pack, ate some beef jerky, and waited. Cowfolk jerky was the best he'd ever tasted, but it was hard to enjoy it now. He sat under the tree, with his back to the rough trunk, shivered and watched the road. Luckily the moon was almost full, and the sky was clear. This made for a cold night, but it was good for his vision. Unluckily, Mae never showed up, not that he had expected her to, not really. It was quite literally a shot in the dark.

As the sun rose the next morning, he was beyond fear. They needed to invent a new word for what he felt. All of his insides were a tangled mess of writhing eels. Every single muscle and joint screamed in pain from sitting against the tree all night. His world was crumbling apart around him. All of his hopes and dreams were shattering like frozen glass. He could almost hear the crisp cracks and tinkles as the shards of his future fell away.

The thought of harm coming to Mae made him physically ill. He forced himself to get up and mount his horse. He just wanted to die, but he had to find her. He decided to ride back toward the village. He supposed that he could have passed her without knowing it. Maybe she had camped off the road, like they used to do. His spirits began to lift at the thought. Of *course*, that's what she did! He probably rode right past her without knowing it. He rode with a light heart, eyes alert for the slightest movement. He wasn't going to miss her again. Their reunion played in his head. He would jump off of Shawnee, and they would run to each other. They would hug and kiss, and wipe away each other's tears.

His heart began to sink back down as he got closer to the village. He had been shouting her name so much that his voice was hoarse. Still he croaked every few minutes.

"Mae!"

Would she hide from him? The thought was absurd, but it kept digging at him. He could have passed her twice and he wouldn't have known it. She would hear the horse coming down the road before he saw her. If she wanted that badly to be away from him, should he just let her go? Would he search all over the place and finally find her, just to hear her say that she didn't love him? That it had all just been a mean joke? The thought brought tears to his eyes.

No, she loved him, and he knew it. His doubts were just his own self esteem playing tricks on him. They were in love, and nothing was going to change that, not ever. He was going to find her, if it cost him his life. What he had told his mother was true. Mae was his life, and he had no use for it without her. He was going to get her back, and he knew just how to do it.

He turned around, dug his heels into his hungry horse and galloped east, letting the cold wind blow away his fear, his self doubt, and his tears.

Chapter Twenty Five

Levin rode his horse hard. The lean hungry mare chewed up the road and spit it out behind her. His heart swelled with affection for the little mare beneath him. In spite of hunger and exhaustion, she ran. She ran through the forest and the fields. She ran through the morning, her swift hooves clapping a rhythm on the hard packed road. She ran past wagons and startled pedestrians. She ran until their destination grew large before them. Shawnee slowed and trotted through the town and up to the gates of Falcon Keep.

The keep was a tall thin structure, like a dagger stabbing into the sky. Shawnee snorted and breathed heavily as they stopped in front of the guards. There were four guards standing on the ground at the gate.

"Halt," one of the guards said, after Levin had already halted.

"I'm here to see Lord Bracken, if he is still alive," Levin said.

"Lord Bracken isn't in the habit of visiting with sweaty travelers," the guard said.

Levin realized that he was sweating, and shivered as a cold breezed blew over him.

"I am Levin Bannerbreaker," he told the guard. "Your lord will not be happy with the person who turns me away."

The guard studied him for a moment, taking in his clothing, his shield, and his horse, and finally jerking his head to one of the other guards. The man turned and ran through the gate. Levin was sure that Shawnee had been the deciding factor. Anyone who rode a horse must be important. After a few minutes, Lord Bracken strode up to the gate. He looked much the same, with a thick fur cloak protecting him from the cold. He did have a slight limp now, and walked with a thick oaken cane.

"Levin! It *is* you," Lord Bracken said. Levin dismounted and walked up to the older man. "I was afraid that you'd died in the ambush."

"I was afraid that the same had happened to you," Levin said.

"They took me prisoner and held me for ransom," the lord said. "Railey, Take his horse to the stable and see that she's taken care of. Tell Kail to walk her dry, then brush and feed her."

"Thank you," Levin said, handing over the reins.

"So you found yourself an appy mare after all," Lord Bracken said.

"It's a long story," Levin said.

"Come," the older man said, and placed a hand on Levin's back. "Let's get inside where it's warm." They walked through the gates and up the steps of the keep. The interior of the small castle was warm and dry. Levin took off his coat and a servant took it from him. Lord Bracken led him over to a pair of large comfortable chairs by the fire. He motioned for Levin to sit in one of them, which he did. It felt fantastic to sit on the soft warm chair. All of his aches and pains drained away, but not his anxiety.

"There is so much to tell, but I don't have time to tell it," Levin began. "To make a long story short, I was on my way here to give you knews of the cowfolk, when my fiance went missing. I have been looking for her since yesterday afternoon. She is probably wanted by the King by now, and I'm worried that someone has taken her. She was in Brookville last time I saw her."

"Myra," Bracken called, and a servant appeared. "Go fetch Sir Haley." The servant turned and disappeared around a corner. "I can send men out to look. If she has been seen they will find out."

"Thank you," Levin said. "I was doing no good on my own. I just want to get her back. If you help me do that, I will be forever in your debt."

A young lady walked into the room carrying a baby wrapped in a blue blanket.

"Good morning," she said.

"Good morning Lanna," Lord Bracken said. "Levin, this is our heiress Lanna. Lanna, this is my squire, Levin Bannerbreaker."

"Pleased to meet you," the young lady said. She was very pretty, with long blond hair and blue eyes. She wore a thick sleeping gown that brushed the floor. Her small toes peaked out beneath the hem.

"Nice to meet you," Levin said.

"Heiress?" Levin asked after she had gone.

"Couples who can't have children hire an heiress to provide them with an heir. We liked her so much that we kept her on as wetnurse," Lord Bracken explained.

"My Lord," Sir Haley said when he entered. The knight was a tall, wiry man, with thick dark hair and a bushy mustache.

"Take ten of your best men," Lord Bracken commanded. "Start in Brookville and scour the countryside. We are looking for a young woman," he turned to Levin, who supplied the description. "She disappeared yesterday. If you find her, bring her straight here, and if you find out where she is, let me know right away."

"Yes My Lord," Sir Haley said, and spun on his heel. His long legs carried him to the door in three steps.

Levin felt as if a weight had been lifted from his shoulders. He had done the right thing. Those men would have a much better chance of finding her than he would alone, still he couldn't sit around doing nothing. He stood and began to excuse himself.

"Nonsense," the lord exclaimed. "I'll not hear of it. If you don't believe that eleven men are enough, I will send out more. You are going to sit here and talk to me."

The older man was right, of course. The only reason he would go out to look, was to make himself feel better. The thing was, it wouldn't help him feel any better. He would be just as miserable and afraid if he were out there looking for Mae. Shawnee deserved a rest as well. Slowly, but obediently, he sat back down.

"Good," Lord Bracken said. "Now tell me the story of how this fair maiden stole the heart of Levin Bannerbreaker."

Levin began to speak. He told his tale, beginning with the ambush, and meeting Mae and Delia. Lord Bracken let him speak without interrupting. Levin told the story in chronological order, only jumping around when he forgot something important. The lord nodded and listened intently. Only after he finished did Lord Bracken speak.

"So, Princess Delia is with the cowfolk, and she's leading them?" the older man asked.

"I think so, but I'm not sure. She is… older than she seems, wiser, more mature. I know that it sounds crazy, to have her leading the cowfolk, but if you spoke to her, you'd understand. It's not as crazy as it sounds."

"If there are as many of them as you say there are, we will be in trouble if they decide to cross the river," Lord Bracken said. There's something else we need to talk about though. I know who your father was. I can tell you more about him, and how he died."

Levin looked up, suddenly interested.

"You remember my father?" he asked.

"Yes," Lord Bracken said, nodding. "He was my first squire. They didn't start giving my squires numbers until the fourth or fifth one. His name was Levin. He died protecting a little girl. She had crawled from beneath a wagon or something, and just appeared there. He had killed a cowman to protect her, but his halberd was stuck in the man's clothing or maybe wedged in some bone. I don't remember exactly how, but he couldn't free his weapon. Another one of the cowfolk came at the girl, and your father attacked him unarmed. He killed the man, but he took grievous wounds, and died there."

Sir Haley came through the front door just then, and Levin sprang to his feet and turned toward the knight.

"We have located her, my Lord. She is bound south for the Orange Keep," the knight said.

"Good work," Lord Bracken said.

Levin turned around to look at him, and he was holding his thick cane like a weapon. Levin spun back around, ready to fight. Was there something that they needed to defend themselves against?

Blackness. The blackness... swam. The blackness... moved. The blackness... hurt. He reached back with somebody else's hand and touched the pulsing knot on the back of his head. Pain lanced through his brain and down his neck. He thought that his vision was blurred, but in the darkness he couldn't really tell. He lost the hand, he couldn't use it anymore. He floated in darkness. He felt empty. The blackness swirled, morphed, and finally coalesced into a familiar figure.

"Levin, your loyalty and strength are wasted on these people. This land will be washed clean and you are at the center of it. You were born low, but you will climb high, but first you must save her, savor... savior.

"Levin."

Someone was doing something to someone else's leg.

"Levin."

No, it was his leg.

"*Levin!*"

He opened his eyes, and saw someone in the dim light. The light was dim, but it seemed too bright in his eyes. The intruder looked familiar, sounded familiar, but he couldn't remember a name.

The man grabbed his arm and pulled him up to a sitting position. His head swam, and he thought he might vomit. He put both of his hands on his head and sat still for a moment, trying to get his bearings.

"That's it son. Take a second, but we don't have long," the stranger said. No, not a stranger, he knew that voice. Master Wayne?

"What's going on," his voice sounded like two pieces of paper being rubbed together.

"Bracken is a snake," Wayne said. "You're in a cell in the back of the stable. I mean to get you out of here. We need to hurry, we don't have all night."

Levin slowly got to his feet. He was having a difficult time understanding the smaller man, but he felt the urgency in his voice. His head throbbed with a pulse of it's own, and it hurt badly. He steadied himself on the other

man's shoulder and allowed himself to be led through the cell door. They
passed a sleeping guard on their way to the stable.

"Old Chail is going to be in trouble in the morning, but there's not help for
it," Wayne said.

Shawnee was already wearing a Murickan saddle and a pair of bulging
saddlebags. Levin's sword belt and shield were leaning against the wall of
her stall.

"They are taking the pretty webinar south, to deliver her to the King.
Bracken switched sides when he was captured. He changes allegiance
like we change shirts," the older man said. "Ride down the South Road,
and you will catch them."

"What about you?" Levin asked. "What will you do?"

"Don't worry about me," Wayne said. "You just get on that horse and get
out of here. I'll be alright."

Levin belted on his sword, picked up his shield, and opened the gate.
Shawnee looked well rested and ready to go. He led her out of the stall
and mounted, with some trouble. His head swam and his stomach was a
mess.

"Thank you," he said to master Wayne.

"I want that girl safe too," Wayne said. "You go and free her before the
King gets a hold of her. The Weaver with you," he said with a touch of
unexpected piety.

"And with you," Levin said, and rode off into the night.

Chapter Twenty Six

Levin rode through the cold early morning, each clop of Shawnee's hooves sending a jolt of pain through his head. He did not ride Shawnee hard, but he did press her to make good time, changing gaits between trot and slow gallop, the miles melted away behind them.

He cursed himself for a Web tangled fool for trusting Lord Bracken. Somehow he should have known. He should have known that nobody could be trusted. That wasn't a lesson that he'd be likely to forget anytime soon. Being stabbed in the back like that made him feel like the kid he was. Just an idiot boy from the country with mud on his boots and grass in his hair.

Levin didn't know how long he had lain in that cell, unconscious, but it couldn't have been more than a few hours, could it? Whoever took Mae couldn't have more than half a day's lead on him. They probably had her tied up in a wagon. He supposed they could have her on a donkey or horse, but that wouldn't be as convenient. If he were going to transport a prisoner over a long haul, he'd want a wagon.

He was thankful when he saw the sun's rays begin to peak out above the horizon. The cold wind made his ears hurt and go numb, in turns. Any warmth would be welcome. The pain in his head was subsiding little by little, thank the Weaver. He reached back under the hood of his cloak and touched the lump. It was roughly the size and shape of a chicken egg cut in half. He winced and sucked in a breath as his fingers sent a jolt of pain through his head. He jerked his hand away, as if burned, and wiped at his watery eyes.

He had no idea how he would go about getting Mae free from her captors. He didn't know how many of them there were, nor did he know how they were traveling. They could be walking, he supposed, but Orange Keep was a long way from here. They were almost certainly mounted. He thought that no matter how they were traveling, or how many of them there were, it would probably be best to go at them at night, while some of them were sleeping. The element of surprise was all he had going for him, and he needed to make the most of it.

At around midmorning he was trotting around a bend in the road, and saw a small man on a small donkey, sitting on the donkey with his arms raised, facing three bowmen that were standing in a line across the road. Bandits. His options flashed through his head, and he knew that he could not allow thieves to take his horse, and he would not run away and allow this little man to be robbed. Levin drew his sword and let Shawnee feel his heels.

"Heeyah," he said to her.

He went straight at the bandits at a gallop. Two of them fled as he flew past the donkey, but one was rooted to his spot. The bowman let loose a shaft that barely missed Levin, which was a fatal mistake. Shawnee reached the thief in two strides and Levin's razor sharp sword took him across the chest. Levin felt ribs break beneath the blade, and had to yank it free from the man's sternum, nearly yanking him from the saddle in the process.

He wheeled the appy mare and waved to the little man.

"Come on, let's go!" Levin shouted.

The wouldbe victim didn't need any more urging. He thumped the little donkey with his boots. The little animal laid it's long ears back and jumped forward with surprising speed. Levin watched to make sure that no one was able to put an arrow in the little stranger's back, but the bandits did not reappear from the woods.

The newly formed pair galloped for a couple of hundred yards, just in case though. Once they slowed, Levin took a moment to look down at the little man. Levin guessed that his new companion was five feet tall, and thin as a reed. He had shaggy brown hair crawling out from under a soft felt cap. His beard was long and shaggy as well. He wore a stout coat, worn, but well cared for. He was a couple of years older than Levin, by the look of him.

"Thank you Sir," the man said. "I'm Herly, and your help is greatly appreciated."

"You're welcome. I'm glad I could help. I'm Levin, but I'm no knight."

The little man looked up at him, puzzled.

"You have the sword and shield of a knight, the trusty steed of a knight, and a knight's vow to help those in need. No one will ever say that ol' Herly didn't show his proper respects. You probably have an earned name too," Herly said.

"Bannerbreaker," Levin mumbled.

"What was that?" Herly asked.

"Bannerbreaker," Levin said more clearly.

"Levin Bannerbreaker, slayer of bandits, and protector of the southern road, and I have only known you for five seconds. Aye Sir Levin, you're a knight alright. Whether some lord or other has patted your shoulder makes no difference to regular folk like me. I know my respects. You're probably on a knight's noble quest no doubt."

"I'm going to rescue my fiance," Levin said. He saw no harm in telling the little man that much.

"Ah, I knew it. I'm on my way south to buy oranges. I'm going to be a trader. I'll buy a cartload of delicious oranges, and take them north to sell for a profit. Erebody I know loves oranges," Herly said.

"Where are you from?" Levin asked.

"The mountains," Herly said. "It's a good place if you like hunting and fishing, but I have bigger dreams. I want to build something, and make something of myself."

Shawnee's hooves went clip clop clip clop on the hard packed road, and now the little donkey's clipclipclipclipclip, was added to the sound of travel. Levin had seen his fair share of donkeys, but this one had the longest ears he'd ever seen. He said as much to the little man.

"Oh aye, Sir Levin," Herly said. "I call him Hearly, cause he can hear so good with those big ears, and cause I'm Herly."

"Call me Levin," Levin said. "You don't have to call me sir." He felt a little uncomfortable being addressed as a knight, like an imposter. He didn't suppose that it would hurt anything out here in the middle of nowhere, but it still bothered him.

"Nawssir," Herly replied. "I know my respects, and you're the first real knight I ever met. I'll be tangled before I talk to you like some commoner."

"But I'm not a *real* knight," Levin said exasperated.

Herly looked at him as if he just claimed that his horse could fly.

"Is that part of your quest?" the little man asked.

"Is what part of my quest?" Levin said.

"Pretending to be common folk. Is that why you're doing it?" Herly said.

"Yes," Levin said, not seeing any other way out of it. "No one can know that I'm a knight." It was kind of true.

"Ok... Levin," Herly said, and winked at him.

Levin reached up to rub his forehead and noticed blood on his hand. He looked at his hand more closely, and found that the blood had run down his arm. He looked up his arm and found a gash in the shoulder of his coat. He pulled Shawnee to a stop and dismounted. He supposed that the archer hadn't completely missed after all. He handed the reins to Herly and took off his coat.

"What's going on?" Herly asked.

"I'm bleeding," Levin said, and pulled his shirt down to inspect the wound. It was a clean cut, but it was still bleeding a little. He grabbed a handful of snow and scrubbed at the blood. He got most of it off without any trouble. He looked through the saddlebags, but couldn't find anything useful, so he cut a strip off of the bottom of his shirt. He wrapped it around the wound and had Herly tie it.

"Get shot by arrows a lot, do ya?" Herly asked once they were on their way again.

"No, that was the first time. I'm not really a knight, you know," Levin said.

"Oh, I know," Herly said, and winked conspiratorially again.

Levin just shook his head.

"Do you mind if I draw you?" Herly asked, as he reached back into a saddlebag and produced a sketching pad. He put his hand into his coat and pulled out a stick of charcoal.

"While you're riding a donkey?" Levin asked.

"Sure, why not. I gots nothin' better to do," Herly said.

Levin shrugged and nodded while the little man looked at him and scratched on the paper. He would close one eye, and look at Levin with his tongue sticking out of the corner of his mouth, then look at the pad and scratch it with the charcoal, or rub it with his thumb. This went on for the better part of an hour. Levin tried to look relaxed, but knew that he was botching it. There's an odd thing that happens when one person tries to draw another from real life. The model is supposed to look relaxed and natural, but being the focus of such scrutiny is stressful, and not conducive to a relaxing pose.

Eventually the little man grunted, held the study out at arms length, and nodded. He spun it around and Levin was stunned. It was a rough work, to be sure, but there was a figure on a horse that could be him and Shawnee. The thing that grabbed his attention was the emotion. The drawing conveyed tiredness, but determination. Levin knew that he couldn't draw that well with a table, proper pencils, and all day to finish.

"That's amazing," he said. "You're gifted. Why aren't you rich, drawing for lords and ladies and such?"

"Your father's got to have the right name for that. My da's a woodcutter. They wouldn't let me through the door, let alone sit down to rub knuckles with me while I draw," he gave a resigned laugh, short and a little bitter. "All the gifts in the Web don't mean nothin' if you ain't got the right name."

The little man tucked his drawing papers away, and Levin reluctantly decided to make camp. The sun was low in the sky by now. He had hoped to catch up to his quarry by now, but he hadn't seen them. He knew that he shouldn't feel rushed. Orange Keep was a long way off. He had plenty of time.

"There's liable to be trouble when I catch up to the one's that has my fiance," Levin said, as they bedded down for the night.

"I reckon I'd be walking or dead, if not for you, so I won't mind a bit of trouble," Herly said.

Levin smiled and nodded. He didn't know how much help the little artist would be when the killing time came, but his company was welcome nonetheless. That night Levin's dreams were filled with blood, and arrows, and steel.

Chapter Twenty Seven

They woke with the sunrise the next morning and set out once more. Herly asked Levin about his past, and Levin felt obliged to tell his story. He told the little artist almost everything, only leaving out the princess. Luckily Herly didn't think to ask him why he went to the cowfolk.

Herly wistled.

"You've done more in the last year, than most folks will do in a whole life," he said. "I've never heard of this Lord Bracken, but he sounds like a proper villain. I'm a wood chopper by trade," Herly said, and shook his head at Levin's sideways glance. "I know that I'm small, but I fashioned a tool to do the chopping, and Hearly here did the carrying. I was able to make a decent living for myself and my wife. She died last winter though, and I decided to do something different. I always hated chopping wood anyway. It's the most boring thing in the Web, I swear."

"I'm sorry to hear about your wife," Levin said. "How did she die?"

A dark cloud came over Herly's face. When he spoke again, the words were strained.

"Sickness got her. She fell ill over the winter, shaking and sweating. Nothing I could do," he said, and began to pick at some invisible bramble on Hearly's ear.

Levin immediately regretted asking the question. If she had died of illness, it meant that she had been unfaithful. What a painful way to lose someone you love. He mentally kicked himself for asking, and made a mental note to never ask that question, of anyone, again.

"I'm sorry," Levin said.

Herly waved a hand in dismissal.

"What's done is done," he said. "She's in Florida now. I'll have some questions for her when I get there, no sense in fretting about it now."

As they rode through the day, talking and getting to know each other, Levin began to realize that he really liked this little man. Herly was smart and friendly, not to mention talented. Levin had always been something of a loner. Not by choice, not really, it had always just been that way. He had always been more comfortable in solitude, until he met Mae. Mae's company didn't chafe like so many others had, and to his surprise, he felt comfortable with this little donkey riding artist as well.

It was late morning when they spotted the other group of people in the distance. From this far away, he couldn't be completely sure, but there seemed to be three mounted riders and a small wagon. He had assumed that there would be a wagon or cart of some sort, to carry Mae. Now he had to decide whether to take the chance of passing them and doubling back, or trailing them until nightfall. If they were spotted trailing them, it could alert their prey. If they passed the other party, they would probably be dismissed as harmless, but they took the chance of being recognized. They stopped and talked it over. There was only one way for Lord Bracken's men to go, so they had no fear of losing them.

"Your horse stands out like a trapped fly," Herly said. "I don't think that it's a good idea to ride past them."

"You're probably right," Levin agreed. "We'll hang back and wait for them to make camp."

They hung back and kept to the edge of the road, so that their silhouettes wouldn't stand out against the white background. They stayed back as far as possible, because the donkeys in the other party could start braying to Hearly. The other party was traveling slowly, so they dismounted and led their animals. They spent the rest of the day trudging through unpacked snow and talking in whispers. When the sun hung low in the sky, the group that they were following stopped and began to make camp. Levin and Herly stayed well behind, and waited for darkness. It would be a long night, with just a sliver of a moon, perfect for going undetected.

Levin tried to remain patient, even though his heart was drumming in his ears. They moved off, deeper into the woods, and tied their mounts to a tree. The snow would muffle the sounds of walking, another good thing. A person could be heard from a good distance when walking on dry summer leaves.

After full dark had settled in, the pair made their way through the woods to the other's camp. It wasn't difficult to find or to observe. The men were careless and unafraid. They had a large fire going already, and two of them had bedded down. Of the other two, one was sitting by the fire, warming his hands, and the other was at the wagon, where the donkeys were tied. Levin and Herly watched the camp for a few minutes, then retreated back to their mounts, to talk.

"I can sneak in and cut their donkeys loose," said Herly. "I'll scare them off. They will take off after the donkeys and then you can go in to get your woman."

"This isn't chopping wood Herly," Levin said. "This is dangerous. You could get killed."

"I've done some other things besides chop wood," Herly said with a mischievous grin. "Plus, tearing into those bandits back there, that was dangerous, and you helped me anyway. I'm not going to stand by or leave you to do this alone. We could have died back there with those bandits, and I reckon we could die here. Anyway, a squire never leaves his knight to fight alone. We are a team."

Squire? He thinks he's my squire, Levin thought. *But I'm no knight!* He had figured that the matter had been settled, but it seemed otherwise. Now was not the time to argue over it though. If Herly was going to help him get Mae back, then he could call himself a squire.

They worked out the details of the plan, and then waited a few hours in silence. Once Levin felt sure that the camp was settled, he told Herly to go ahead. The small man ran off, silently, melting into the shadows. Levin went back the way that hey had gone to scout. He settled down and waited for Herly to do his part.

Levin mentally prepared himself for what he was about to do. If he had one gift from the Weaver, it was the ability to force himself to do a thing. One time when he was ten or twelve years old, he and about a dozen other kids went to the cliff at Lady Creek, and decided to jump off. About half of the children weren't afraid of heights, and just jumped. The other half were afraid, Levin included. He was the only scared kid who jumped. He wanted to know if he could do it, so even though he was afraid, he forced himself off of the ledge. He ended up belly flopping and nearly drowned, but he had overcome his fear, and made himself do it. When the other kids tried to get him to go again, they jeered him for being a coward when he refused, even the kids who were too afraid to jump in the first place, to his astonishment. But he didn't have to prove anything else to himself, so their peer pressure had no effect on him.

That is what he did now. He was afraid, but his Uncle Remi's words came back to him. "Bravery is action in spite of fear, son," his uncle had told him. "Action instead of fear is called stupidity." He knew that it was ok to be afraid, but he also knew that he couldn't allow the fear to control him. He closed his eyes and pushed the fear away. When he opened them, he was calm and breathing steadily.

There was a shout, and the man on guard took off at a run. One of the sleeping men bounded to his feet and followed. Levin swallowed hard, and ran into the camp. He chopped the neck of the other sleeper. It wasn't honorable, but it was effective. Blood fountained, but the man didn't make a sound. He turned and started toward the wagon, and standing there was Cholt. The big man had a shield, a spear, and a malevolent grin.

"By the Weaver's crooked dick," he said. "Look who we have here."

Levin said nothing. He gripped his father's sword and attacked. He kept a defensive mindset though, he needed to gauge the bigger man, without getting himself killed. He had beaten Cholt when they fought hand to hand, but they both knew that the fight was evenly matched. It could have gone the other way if the bigger man had landed one solid punch. He had beaten Cholt soundly, but not easily, and now the man was eager for revenge. The sight of the shield he'd stolen enraged him even more, when he saw it on Levin's left arm. Cholt knew that the cowfolk shield should be his, and he'd take it off of Levin's corpse this time.

Cholt blocked Levin's cuts and trusts with his shield, and countered with 18 inches of razor sharp spear head. Levin felt the impact on his shield as the big man thrust and swung. Levin countered and moved to his left, keeping his shield in front of him, and searching for a weakness in his opponent's defense. Like himself though, Cholt was a warrior, a fighter, a killer.

"You're gonna die Bannerboy," Cholt hissed.

Levin said nothing. Sweat ran down his face, and he knew that he was running out of time. The others would return with the donkeys any minute. This was his one, and most likely his only, chance to free Mae. He had to end this quickly. He took a swing at the bigger man and exposed a gap in his left side. Cholt saw it and lunged. Levin tried to bring his shield down to block it, but he wasn't fast enough. He felt the steel peirce his flesh, just beneath his ribs. As he had hoped though, the move left Cholt vulnerable. Levin brought his father's sword down, much as Herly had swung his axe to chop wood, and cut through the base of the bigger man's skull. He heard the bone crunch and felt the scrape through the handle of the sword.

Cholt fell to the ground, and twisted the spear in doing so. Levin cursed as pain lanced through him, and dropped his sword. He grabbed the spear and pulled it out, blood flowed out of the hole it left. Levin picked up his sword and hurried over to the wagon. He pulled back the covering, and there she was, cold and shivering, but alive! He had never felt such relief. Wincing with pain, he reached in and cut her bonds, and removed the gag, then helped her out of the wagon.

"You're hurt," she said.

"It doesn't matter," Levin said through clenched teeth. "Let's go."

He grabbed her by the arm and led her back to the spot where he had left Shawnee. To his surprise, Herly was standing there with another donkey. He didn't want to take the time for explanations. He just helped Mae onto the new mount and then untied Shawnee.

"We need to get out of here," he told them after he'd mounted.

He kept close to Mae as they rode through the night. It would be tomorrow morning before the other men found out which way they had gone, and then there was a good chance that they wouldn't follow. He had killed two of them after all. That left one soldier and a wagon driver. They wouldn't be itching to chase his party down.

The pain in his side was intense, but he did his best to push it out of his mind. There was not time to worry about it, and there wasn't much they could do for the injury anyway. He looked over at Mae every few seconds, maybe to verify that she was really there, that this wasn't a dream, or maybe just because he liked to look at her. They rode through the night, cross country, staying off of the road. Levin knew that Lady Creek ran west to east from the mountains. If they kept going north, they would eventually run into it, and he could find his way home from there.

Chapter Twenty Eight

As soon as the sun rose in the morning, Mae insisted on stopping and checking his wound. She had him stay mounted, so as not to get it bleeding again from movement. Blood already soaked his pants and saddle, which made riding extremely uncomfortable, but there wasn't much he could do about it. She pulled his shirt up and inspected it. She smelled it and told him that she didn't believe that any of his organs had been punctured.

"I could be wrong," she said. "You need to be careful." She cut some more material from his shirt, and from her own, and made a makeshift dressing for the wound. It had stopped bleeding, but she said that the covering would help to keep it clean.

"Thank you, thank you both for getting me away from them," she said, after she had remounted and they were moving once more.

"I have been worried sick to death since you left," Levin said. "I would never give up until I got you back."

"I'm Herly," Herly said. "I'm Sir Levin's squire. It's nice to meet ya Mae."

"Squire?" Mae looked at Levin with a raised eyebrow.

"I'll explain later," Levin said. He was too tired and miserable to get into it right then, sitting in a pool of his own blood and clenching his teeth against the pain in his side.

"I was on my way south to be a trader," Herly continued, "but I've decided to become a knight like Sir Levin. Sir Herly, has a nice ring to it, don't you think?" It was funny to hear the little man talk this way. He had to be four or five years Levin's senior, but he sounded like a youngster looking up to his hero. "Sir Levin rescued me from some bandits," he went on. "Hearly too, they would have taken him for sure. He even got shot with an arrow saving us."

"You got shot?" Mae asked Levin.

Levin shrugged and used his chin to motion to the slice in his coat sleeve.

"It's just a scratch," he managed to say. The knot on the back of his head started to ache. He turned to Mae to tell her about the bandits, and the trees around him, sort of slipped or blurred. He closed his eyes to steady his vision and clear his head.

When he opened them again, he was looking straight up at the sky. The sun was too low on the horizon. He blinked and looked around. Herly was sitting by a fire, cooking some fish that were skewered on sticks. Was he dreaming? He tried to say Herly's name, but what came out was half croak and half rattle. Herly looked over at him, in surprise.

"Mae, he's awake!" Herly called.

Levin heard her footsteps coming from the other direction and turned to look at her, or tried to. The pain in his side was intense. Her face came into view as she knelt down over him.

"Lie still," Mae said. She put a hand on his forehead and raised his shirt to look at his wound. "You have a nasty bump on your head, along with the stab wound and the arrow scratch. Your scratch should have been sewn shut, and you are probably dizzy and nauseous from the head wound."

He nodded, slowly, it seemed to be the safest thing to do. Mae got up and walked over to the fire. She grabbed a couple of sticks and brought them over to him. They smelled delicious and he realized how hungry he was.

"You need to eat something," Mae said, and started tearing off pieces of steaming flesh. She blew on the flaky white pieces to cool them before she put them into his mouth. He ate greedily and gratefully.

"How long have I been asleep?" he managed to ask between bites.

"Two days," Mae said.

"Mother's milk," he said, and started to get up. She put a hand on his shoulder and pushed him back down.

"We're fine," she said. "Everything's fine, and you need to rest. It won't do us any good to have you fall out of your saddle again. You scared a ghost into Shawnee, and it took Herly an hour to fetch her back. We'll rest here for a little while longer, just until you get some strength back, then we'll be on our way."

Levin reluctantly laid back down after drinking some water that Mae had put to his lips. She was right of course. The reasons for going were outweighed by the reasons for resting. He took a look around and saw that they had moved him to a good spot by a small stream. The sound of the babbling water was relaxing. He thanked Mae for the food and water, then closed his eyes. Sleep was a welcome respite from the pain.

It was dark when he opened his eyes again. The campfire was burning low, and the stars were sparkling in the clear sky. He felt the back of his head. The knot was there, but a bit smaller, and the pain had lessened by quite a bit. It was still sore to the touch, but it felt much better. Then he touched the wound at his side. There was a rough scab under the loose bandage. It itched a little but still hurt badly when he moved.

He laid back and closed his eyes again. He laid there for a long while, and began to worry that he might not be able to get back to sleep. Then Mae was shaking his shoulder, and he opened his eyes into a bright sunny sky.

"Your fever is gone and your wounds are looking a lot better," she said. "Do you feel strong enough to get up?"

"Yeah, I think so," Levin answered.

He rolled over to his side and paused when his head began to swim. After the dizzy spell subsided he pushed himself to his knees and stood slowly. Mae grabbed his arm to keep him steady. He was still weak, but he felt good. Herly was cooking fish again. Levin's stomach growled audibly.

"Go get something to eat," Mae said.

He walked slowly to the fire and sat down next to Herly. The little man inspected the fish, and handed the best looking one to Levin, who burned the roof of his mouth eating it. While he started in on the next one, Mae brought over some more sticks with fish on them, and Herly placed them over the fire to cook. Levin was positively famished and ate what must have been over a dozen of the small silver fish. They had a light smokey flavor and white flaky flesh, delicious. He felt better, seemingly with every bite.

"Where'd you get all of the fish?" Levin asked.

"Mae found a beaver dam upstream. There are all kinds of them there. She says that they aren't afraid of her and they're easy to catch," Herly said.

Levin looked over at the woman for whom he'd risked so much. He had been so afraid that he'd never see her again. His heart swelled at the sight of her, going around the camp, gathering things up.

"Do you feel strong enough to travel?" she asked, looking over at him.

"Yeah, I think so," he said, and got up to prove it. He walked over to Shawnee and began to scratch her spotted shoulder.

"Good," Mae said. "Let's get packed up and back on our way."

The two men did as she bid them. Levin managed to get Shawnee saddled without too much trouble. Getting the bridle over her ears proved to be too painful though, and he had to ask Mae for help. That was another thing about her. He never felt ashamed or inadequate around her. She loved him for who he was, good or bad, right or wrong. They had spent too many days traveling, with just each other for company, not to know each other inside and out. She knew all of his flaws and he hers.

Once the bridle was in place, Levin grabbed her arms and pulled her in for a kiss. This kiss was even better than the first one. It had the weight of time, it was flavored with past hurts and laughter, sadness and triumph, calluses and tenderness, but underneath it all was a foundation of love. It was an amazing experience to literally hold his life in his hands, to feel her lips, and hear her breathing. She was everything.

Their kisses seemed to last forever, but were always over too soon for him. He pulled away, this time fully aware of the sadness that was always there at the breaking of their embrace. He held her at arm's length and looked into her eyes for several heartbeats.

"I love you," he said. "Don't ever leave me again, no matter what anyone says."

"I won't," Mae said, feeling more than a little foolish at the trouble she had caused. She had left for him, to save him from a decade of loneliness, because his mother had made sense. Now though, it felt completely selfish. He had risked his life to get her back, and her self loathing was only eclipsed by her love for him.

They mounted up and headed north once more, treasuring every moment that the Weaver gave them.

Chapter Twenty Nine

The rest of the trip was uncomfortable for Levin, even though Mae had cleaned the blood from his saddle and britches while they were camped at the stream. Every step that the horse took was painful, if no longer agonizing. He had a feeling that Herly was going to be surprised when the little man found out that Levin didn't live in a castle, with servants. Herly had turned out to be a loyal and faithful friend, and Levin was glad for his company. It was close to midday, and they were listening to Herly's second story so far.

"So the fella just picked up the sheep, and took off running down the road," Herly said, animatedly telling the story. "Me and Tory just looked at each other. Neither one of us wanted to look like a fool, chasing this guy down the road, but we couldn't just let him run off with Bertha. You wouldn't' think that a fella would be able to run very fast, while carrying a full grown sheep, but let me tell you, that guy ran like the Weavers weasel was on his tail. We finally caught him, but everyone in town called us 'The Sheep Chasers' for the rest of the winter."

Levin and Mae looked at each other as Herly laughed at his own story. The artist was full of those kinds of stories. They would ride along in silence for a while talking occasionally, and Herly would break out into a long winded tale. Sometimes they were funny, but mostly they were little more than slightly interesting, and just a bit better than silence. He had an inexhaustible supply of them though, and neither Levin nor Mae told him to stop.

So they passed the time listening to Herly's stories and to the rhythmic sounds of hooves in the snow. Eventually Levin spotted a cliff in the distance. The same cliff that he'd leapt from as a child. They had made it to Lady Creek. They weren't far from home now. Home created a different set of problems for him. Lord Bracken would probably come looking for them, and he'd have an army with him. It all depended on the two survivors that he'd left. If they found their donkeys and then went straight back to Falcon Keep, Lord Bracken already knew of the rescue, and might be waiting at Brookville already.

If, on the other hand, they couldn't find the donkeys that Herly had turned loose, they would have to walk back, and that could take a week or more. All of that is based on the supposition that they would return to face the punishment of losing their captor. They could very well choose to avoid punishment by going somewhere else. Levin figured that they had a 50/50 chance at best.

"I should have taken care of those other two men," Levin said aloud, to himself as much as to anyone else.

"You had a spear in your side, remember," Mae said, a little exasperated. They had already been over this a time or two. "You couldn't have done anything more."

"I just don't want to spend the rest of my life running and hiding from Bracken," Levin said.

"We'll figure something out. Just try to relax and be happy that you got me away from them," Mae said. "*I'm* sure happy that you did."

Levin nodded, he knew that she was right, but it was difficult not to worry. Getting her away from the soldiers was great, but he felt the need to protect her for the rest of her life. He knew that she felt the same way about him, so why wasn't she worried about it? It amazed him, when he thought about it, how different people could be. She would worry and fret over a hole in his shirt, and pester him until he took it off so she could mend it, but an evil lord hunting them for the rest of their lives? No problem. Won't give it a second thought.

It was near dusk by the time they reached Lady Creek, so they decided to make camp. The only place to cross the water was downriver, and that would take them away from Brookvilled. There was no way that they'd make it to the village this evening. Seeing the cliff again took Levin back to the last time he had thought about it, and to the fight immediately after. The act of killing the sleeping man weighed on him. He told himself that he didn't have a choice, and that was true, but he still felt more than a little shame for killing a sleeping man. If he hadn't done it, he'd more than likely be dead, and Mae would still be on her way to Orange Keep. He played through it again in his mind's eye, but the bottom line was that the sleeping man had abducted his fiance, and had paid the price for it.

"You ok?" Mae asked.

"Huh," Levin said, looking around. He hadn't noticed that Shawnee had stopped walking. "Oh yeah, I was just thinking."

"If you two want to get a fire going, I'll see about getting us some fish," Mae said.

He unsaddled Shawnee, then fed her and tied her to a tree. He was glad that they were almost home, he was almost out of grain. Then he set to gathering firewood. They were all tired and made camp quietly. Herly was already asleep by the time Levin laid his bedroll out next to Maes. Lying down felt good to Levin, his sore muscles and aching injuries needed rest. Just as he closed his eyes, Mae spoke.

"Levin, we need to talk," she said quietly.

"About what?" he asked, rolling over on his side to look at her.

"I am very grateful that you saved me, but I can't help but think about what your mother said," Mae answered.

"She was wrong," he said, his voice tight.

"You're going to be alone after I die, maybe for a long time," she said.

"I'd rather have a few years of true love, than none. Everyone dies for all sorts of reasons. There's no guarantee that you'll die before me, or if I found someone else, that they'd live longer than you," Levin said.

"Don't you ever think about our age difference?" Mae asked.

"Only when you bring it up. It never crosses my mind otherwise. There's no reason to think about it. I know that I love you, that's all I need to know. Either you love me or you don't," Levin said.

"You know I love you," Mae said. "It's just that it's hard being almost the same age as your mother."

"Yeah, I suppose it is, but we can't live our lives by what anyone else thinks. Not even my mother. You are marrying me, not her. Our love, and our life together are the only things that matter. Nothing else," Levin said.

"I know you're right," Mae said. "I just need to talk about it sometimes. I need to reassure myself that you really love me, and that I'm doing the right thing. I am leaving the bethel to start a family with you."

"I haven't forgotten, and I know that you are giving up a lot. I will make sure that you never regret it," Levin said. "I love you Mae."

"I love you Levin."

They kissed and fell asleep in each other's arms.

Chapter Thirty

It was still early in the morning and Penny was outside sweeping the steps when they rode up. At first she didn't recognize her son. The little girl's words came back to her. "He will return to you, but you won't recognize him," she had said. It was true, her little boy was gone. Hunger and fighting had erased the soft youthful lines of his face and drawn hard angles in their place. His wonderful green eyes had lost their innocence. He carried his father's sword as if it were a part of him, and maybe it was.

Still, her heart leapt at the sight of them. She felt horrible for what she'd said to Mae. She realized now that it was none of her business, and she just hoped that they'd be able to forgive her. Levin dismounted and walked up to her.

"I love you mom," he said, and gave her a hug.

"I'm so sorry," Penny said to both of them, as tears ran down her face. "I'm so sorry."

"It's ok," Levin said, and stepped back away from her.

Mae stepped up and hugged her next. Penny was thankful for the overture. She hugged Mae tightly and apologized for what she'd said. Levin loved this woman, so Penny would love her too.

"Mom," Levin said. "This is Herly."

"His squire," Herly finished, and opened his arms for a hug. Penny hugged the little man and looked over at Levin questioningly, but he only smiled and shrugged.

Penny brought them all inside, and got them seated, then set to making coffee for everyone. Levin noticed that there was an additional chair at the table.

"Uncle Remi make another chair?" Levin asked his mother.

"Yes," she answered. "He didn't like it that people had to stand last time you were here. He said that it made him feel guilty. He's got another one on the way."

Levin sat down in the new chair to admire his uncle's handiwork. The chair was plain but sturdy.

Penny brought the coffee around and sat cups down in front of each of them, along with the last of the sugar. It wouldn't have lasted much longer anyway. Hopefully the next trader to pass through will have some for sale. Levin was the only one who put sugar in his coffee, she noticed. The other two drank it black. Most of the time, people drank their coffee black. Sugar was an expensive luxury. She'd heard that noblefolk put cream in their coffee. She'd always wondered what that tasted like. It must be nice to be rich.

Penny took the empty chair and put a little sugar in her cup. She watched as the other three tasted their coffee and smiled, then waited for one of them to begin.

"We're getting married tomorrow," Levin said. Penny took a sip of coffee to hide her surprise. "Lord Bracken will be hunting us." He raised his hand to forstall what Penny was about to say. "It would have happened anyway. He changed sides, now he's hunting the princess instead of protecting her. He was looking for us when this happened. Anyway," he went on, "we are going to get married here before we leave. We either have to go somewhere safe, or raise an army of our own to defeat Bracken," he said, and chuckled at the obvious hopelessness of the latter option.

"Where will you go?" Penny asked.

"We don't know yet," it was Mae who answered.

"Well," Penny paused and took a deep breath. "I need to apologize to the both of you." Levin and Mae both started to protest, but Peny raised a hand and waved them to silence. "I have been scared to death since the day you left. You're uncle Remi helped me to see that what I did was selfish. I did what I did, because I was afraid of losing my son, but when the two of you left, I realized that I couldn't control it. You two deserve an apology, and I hope I deserve your forgiveness," she said looking down at the table, much in the same way that Levin had on the day he was drafted.

They both got up from the table, but it was Mae who got to her first and wrapped her in a warm embrace.

"Of course you are forgiven," Mae said quietly. "I only hope that I am as good a mother as you are, when I'm in your position."

Levin wrapped his arms around both of them and said, "I love you."

The door opened, and Uncle Remi entered holding a new chair. Aunt Tilda was right behind him. Levin stood up, walked over to his Uncle and gave him a hug, then embraced his Aunt.

"Uncle Remi, Aunt Tilda, this is my friend Herly," Levin said, gesturing to the little man who was sitting at the table.

"I'm Sir Levin's squire," Herly said, getting up and bowing slightly.

"I thought only knights had squires," Tilda said.

"It's a long story," Levin replied.

"I see that I still don't have enough chairs," Remi said, placing the new chair at the table. He motioned for Tilda to take a seat, and she did. Levin stood leaning against the counter and insisted that his Uncle Remi take the seat at the head of the table.

Penny was happy and let her tears of joy flow. It warmed her heart to see everyone home and safe, even if it was just temporary. After some very little prodding from Levin, Herly began telling his story, beginning from Levin's attack on the bandits, and ending with seeing Penny on the porch.

There were exclamations of surprise at points of the story that told of Levin's injuries. His mother and aunt kept interrupting and making sure that he was ok, but his Uncle Remi just looked at him and smiled a proud smile. *I have always felt sorry for myself for not having a father*, Levin thought, *and he has been here the whole time, building chairs and making sure that I didn't want for anything.* His uncle blurred and Levin wiped at his eyes.

"Me and Mae are getting married tomorrow," Levin said. "I'm going to go spread the word."

"I'll help," Herly said, getting up.

"Ok," Levin said, and walked to the door. Technically, people could marry in private, but the more people who heard the couple's words, the more official the wedding. It was also commonly felt that more witnesses brought the couple good fortune. He had witnessed several weddings in his life, and they had all been happy affairs with many people. Everyone was normally given much more notice than this though, so Levin wasn't sure how it would turn out. He had heard that they had webinars lead the ceremonies in larger towns. He didn't know why. It seemed to him that the commitment was between two people, not three.

"We'll be back in an hour or so," Levin said, as he closed the door.

They went from house to house, and from establishment to establishment, telling everyone that there was going to be a wedding tomorrow. Most people seemed surprised and happy. A wedding was a great way to break the monotony of winter, even if it was on short notice. They came to the house where Mar used to live. Levin debated with himself whether or not to knock on the door, and finally decided to do it. Not inviting Mar's family seemed cruel to him. He took a deep breath and walked up the steps. When he spoke to Mar's mother she burst into tears and slammed the door in his face.

"What was that about?" Herly asked.

"Her son was drafted with me. He died in our first battle," Levin said. He wondered if she somehow blamed him for Ban's death, or if the sight of him just reminded her. Now was not the time to find out. He wanted to do something for the woman, to ease her pain, but he had no idea where to begin.

Cain Tender, the tavern owner, promised to tell everyone who came by, as did Tether the store keep. His heart sank a little when he saw old lady Tarly's house. Someone had moved in there. He didn't know how he felt about that. He should be happy, he supposed. He knocked on the door, and was greeted by a young woman holding a baby. He told her about the wedding, and moved on.

Herly talked as they walked, but Levin's mind was far away. He thought about Lord Bracken and how long it might be before he showed up with his army. He thought about supporting a family. He had been a soldier when all this began, but now what was he? He couldn't expect Mae to feed them. He had to figure out what to do for a living, but even more importantly, he needed to figure out where to live.

"Sir Levin."

The longer he stayed here, the more danger his family was in.

"Sir Levin!" Herly shouted.

"What?" Levin asked, and looked at Herly, who was pointing east, down the road.

Levin followed the small man's extended arm, and saw his greatest fears come to life. Two columns of soldiers marched towards them from the east. He immediately turned and ran back toward his uncle's house, yelling for people to get out of town. A couple of doors opened and heads peeked out, but that was all. He didn't have time to evacuate the entire town. These people would die, and it would be his fault. He could let Bracken take him, to spare the town, but he couldn't allow them to take Mae. He saw no way out of it. He would not die peacefully in his old age, and go to Florida. His people were going to die, and he would die protecting them. He turned toward the advancing columns and drew his sword.

"Run," he told Herly. "Get out of here."

"A squire never runs," Herly said. Levin didn't have the heart to remind the little man that he wasn't a squire. If Levin could choose his manner of death, then Herly could do the same. Let him die a squire.

And so it was, that an ex squire and a wannabe squire faced down an army, on a chilly winter afternoon, in the middle of Brookville.

Chapter Thirty One

Levin and Herly stood there in silence for a few heartbeats watching the army advance towards them, when Herly turned and ran off, without a word, leaving Levin to face the enemy alone. *Good*, Levin thought. *I didn't want him to die anyway.* Still, it was a completely different experience, facing the army alone. The thought of running slipped through his mind again, and again he dismissed it. Bracken knew that his family lived here, they would never be safe as long as the Lord hunted him. It would be better to die fighting and get it over with. He steeled his nerve and straightened his back.

Then Levin heard footsteps running up behind him. He turned to see Herly handing him his cowfolk shield. He'd left it with the rest of his gear. In the small man's other hand was his knife.

"You are the best squire I've ever had," Levin told him earnestly. "And that's the Father's own truth." Herly nodded and grinned, then turned to face the army that was stopping about a hundred paces away. "I'm sorry that a good death is the only payment I can give you."

"A lot of people don't get that," Herly said. "I'd rather die here with you, than in some other way."

Lord Bracken rode up to the head of the column and dismounted. Levin heard a door slam, and more footsteps and his uncle Remi appeared at his side, carrying a wood axe. Next Ban's mother came with a cleaver, and master Tender carrying an old sword. Aunt Tilda, Mae, and his mother joined the group, along with most of the townsfolk present that day.

Levin's heart swelled with pride for his people, but at the same time he was afraid for them. He was trying to protect them, not get them slaughtered in a battle against armed and armored soldiers. He loved them all at that moment, and hated himself for bringing this down on them.

"I need the webinar," Lord Bracken said in a loud voice, as he walked out into the opening between the two groups. "The King has asked for her, and in the name of the King, I demand that you give her to me. Do this, and we will be on our way. I didn't come here to kill a bunch of store clerks and handmaids, but that is exactly what I will do, if you don't turn her over."

It was Uncle Remi who said, "She's one of us, and we don't *turn over* our own. Go back to where you came, or there will be more blood than you reckoned for."

"This is your last chance," Lord Bracken said. "Once it begins, no quarter will be given. I will leave this place in ashes." He waited a few moments, but no one spoke.

"I will go with him," Mae said.

"No," Levin shouted, along with half a dozen other voices. He looked around trying to find her in the crowd, and saw something moving in the distance.

"Stop," Levin shouted again. "Look," he pointed at the columns of cowfolk drawing near. They stopped and several of them dismounted. The Brookvillers parted to make room. Levin recognized Delia right away. He stared at her in surprise as she walked up to him, trailed by dozens of cowfolk warriors.

"Levin Bannerbreaker," Delia said. "I've come for my due and proper."
She turned to her warriors and ordered them to get the civilians to safety,
then faced Lord Bracken. "I am Delia Frostborn, Heart of the Herd, and
rightful Queen of Muricka. I am afraid that I cannot accept your allegiance,
because you cannot be trusted to serve faithfully. You must be destroyed."

The look on Lord Bracken's face started out as contemptuous self
assurance, and melted into disbelieving dread. He turned and scrambled
back onto his horse and ordered the attack. His men weren't so sure of
themselves, as they had been earlier, but they advanced slowly.

Delia melted back into the crowd, and was replaced by cowfolk warriors,
carrying shields and bowie knives. Levin had time to make sure, with a
quick look around, that all of the civilians had moved back out of the way.
Levin moved in front of Herly, and pushed him toward the rear. Without a
shield, he could only die in a shield wall.

Levin and the cowfolk sprinted the last 10 paces, screaming ululating
battle cries as they smashed into Bracken's troops. The enemy was driven
back, Levin's sword hacked pieces out of shield and body alike. The
bloodlust was on him. There was nothing like seeing the mortal fear in
another man's eyes, nothing. He felt the now familiar surge of life through
his veins, where he walked the tight line between sanity and madness.
When the battle lust had him, life and death were so close, so tightly woven
in the Web, it was hard to tell where one left off and the other began.

He blocked a spear thrust with his shield, and stabbed a man through the
throat. His father's sword was alive in his hands. He swung, thrust, and
chopped until his arm was numb. The jarring impacts on his shield rattled
his bones. He stepped over the dead, in pursuit of the living. The battle
was everything, it consumed Levin's world. It seemed as if it would never

end, and as if it had always been. In that brutal little pocket of eternity, time seemed to stretch like spider's silk, sticky and soft.

His cowfolk companions were just as lethal. They fought with the fury of a storm. The long knives flicked out with deadly accuracy, stealing life like the plague. Their lythe bronze bodies moved with a delicate grace. They looked, almost, to be dancing.

At the end, Bracken's troops broke and ran. They had killed at least half of the Murickan soldiers, fifty or so, but not even half a dozen cowfolk lay dead. He watched Lord Bracken gallop away on his black stallion, and turned to get Shawnee.

Delia was standing there waiting for him.

"Don't worry about him. I have people waiting for him. I knew that he wouldn't stand and fight to the end," she said.

"Father's bushy beard," Levin said. "You saved us!" He picked up the little girl and hugged her. She responded as she always had when he showed her affection, with disinterest. He laughed and spun her around before setting her back down.

"No, you saved me," Delia said. "I'm just taking back what is mine by right."

He left her there to check on his family, and Herly. They were all alive, though Herly had sustained a wound on his right arm. Mae was tending it when Levin found them. She looked over Levin, but found nothing more than a few scrapes and bruises. Everyone wanted to hug him, probably to reassure themselves that he was unhurt.

"You've got some interesting friends," Uncle Remi said, laughing.

A cowfolk warrior patted Levin's shoulder as she walked by, and nodded her head in respect. All of the cowfolk seemed to be setting up camp on the eastern side of town, the way that Bracken had gone. Levin closed his eyes and said a quick prayer of thanks to the Weaver. His family and his town were safe.

Levin donated the services of their three horses to the burial detail. A group of volunteers dug a mass grave out of town, and was dragging the bodies to it. Levin did not envy them, the digging would be tough in the frozen ground. The crows were already starting to investigate though, and leaving the bodies overnight was not an option.

"I almost got one," Herly said. Levin turned to look at him. Mae had done a good job with the bandage.

"Looks like one almost got you," Levin said, pointing to the bandage.

"That?" Herly asked. "No, I tripped and fell on a sword," he said sheepishly, and shrugged.

"Well, you're alive. You survived your first battle," Levin said. "That's all that matters."

"Yeah, I did, didn't I? I survived a battle," the little man said, smiling and standing up straighter.

They spent the rest of the day cleaning up and went to sleep early. Levin felt as if all of the energy had been leached out of him. He slept dreamlessly and peacefully.

Chapter Thirty Two

With the addition of the cowfolk, the wedding was the largest that Brookville had ever seen. This bode well for the couple. Their good fortune was assured with this many well wishers. Master Tender rolled a couple of barrels of beer into the street, and the community made a celebration of it. They celebrated the new couple's health and happiness, but they also celebrated life. They were alive. Life is worth celebrating, especially in the middle of winter, and especially after a battle.

Mae looked beautiful in the powder blue dress that Penny had given her. Levin found some clean clothes to wear. They were a little small, but they were free from blood stains, so they would serve. Mae, Penny, and Tilda thought that he looked handsome.

Levin got down on his knees, took Mae's hands and said, loud enough for everyone to hear, "I choose this woman Mae, as my wife. There will be no other, can be no other, for the rest of my life. I pledge to honor and protect her, to love and defend her, no matter what comes." To Mae he said, "I promise to love you and only you for the rest of my life. I will never give up on you, and I will never abandon you. You are my heart and soul, you are everything, you are my life."

Penny placed a pillow at Levin's feet, for Mae to kneel on. Mae took his hands and went to her knees. She was the most beautiful thing he'd ever seen. There were tears in her eyes when she said, "I take this man Levin Bannerbreaker to be my husband. There will be no other, can be no other, for the rest of my life. I pledge to honor and protect him, to love and defend him, no matter what comes." To Levin she said, "I pledge to love you and only you, until I die. I will stand by you and always be with you, no matter what. You are my heart and soul."

Mae stood, and the people around them cheered as they kissed. Then the crowd parted and Levin saw Delia walking toward him. The little princess was dressed in a snow white buckskin dress, and carried a hew staff. She had a solemn look on her face.

"Kneel," she said to Levin. "Kneel," she said again to Mae.

The couple knelt obediently, giving each other a quick questioning glance. The princess stepped in front of Mae, and placed the staff on her shoulder.

"Mae," she said. "You protected me at great risk to yourself. You got me across the Big Sip, and to the Plainsmen to fulfill my destiny. Yesterday, you were willing to sacrifice yourself for the people of this village. The Hardlands are full of people like these, true and strong, and they deserve a good leader, willing to sacrifice for them. Mae, I would name you my High Webinar. "

Mae looked up at her, disbelievingly, but Delia continued.

"This is a great honor, but it is also a great task. I know that you will do your best for these people. You will take up residence in Falcon Keep, with me." She turned to Levin and placed the staff on his shoulder. "Levin Bannerbreaker, Wogbane, Savior, and Defender of the Innocent, you protected me without concern for your personal safety. You constantly place others above yourself, and do what you know is right. You defended me from all harm, be it beast or man, and delivered me safely to my destiny with the Plainsmen. I, with all of the authority of the Murickan throne, name you Captain of my army, and Defender of Muricka. You also will take up residence at Falcon Keep, with your wife. You have three days to rest and say your goodbyes."

With that, she left them. All of the cowfolk followed her. They dismantled their camp, and were gone within the hour. After receiving congratulations from everyone, and hearty hugs from his uncle Remi, and Herly, Levin took Mae to the place that he'd picked out to build their home. The beaver pond was frozen, but it was just as beautiful as he remembered. Mae loved it too. They spent the day making plans, talking about the future, and making love under the winter sky. Levin had never imagined that there could be so much happiness in all the world.

If they hadn't been so wrapped up in each other, they might have noticed the shadowy figure peering through the bushes, watching them, and they might have heard the hoofbeats growing fainter in the distance.